Wings *of* HOPE

A Father's Story

Henry Plett

HERALD PRESS
Waterloo, Ontario
Scottdale, Pennsylvania

Canadian Cataloguing in Publication Data
Plett, Henry, 1942-
  Wings of hope
ISBN 0-8361-3527-X

1. Plett, Roxanne. 2. Liver—Transplantation—Patients
—Biography. 3. Liver—Transplantation—Religious aspects.
I. Title.

RD546.P54 1990   362.1'9755'6'092   C90-094007-7

The paper used in this publication meets the minimum require-
ments of American National Standard for Information Sciences—
Permanence of Paper for Printed Materials, ANSI Z39.48-1984.

Except as otherwise indicated, Scripture is taken from the
Revised Standard Version of the Bible, copyright © 1946, 1952, 1971,
1973, by the Division of Christian Education of the National
Council of the Churches of Christ in the USA. Used by permis-
sion. Scripture designated KJV is from the King James Version of
The Holy Bible.

WINGS OF HOPE
Copyright © 1990 by Herald Press, Waterloo, Ont. N2L 6H7
  Published simultaneously in the United States by Herald
  Press, Scottdale, Pa. 15683. All rights reserved.
Library of Congress Catalog Card Number: 90-82600
International Standard Book Number: 0-8361-3527-X
Design and cover art by Paula M. Johnson

97 96 95 94 93 92 91 90 10 9 8 7 6 5 4 3 2 1

To Roxanne
for the pain that she endured
for the ordeal we were allowed to share with her
for the bond of love which developed
for the growth which she helped us experience

Foreword

I have lived with the science of organ transplants for a number of years. My brother, Dr. Cal Stiller, is Chief of the Multi-Organ Transplant Service, University Hospital, London, Ontario. Early in his medical career he decided to make organ transplants central to his work.

However, it was only after reading one of his stories of organ transplants that I decided to enter into a project in which he and I would coauthor a book on organ transplants. *Lifegifts*, published by Stoddard in 1990, is the result of that decision.

As a Christian, I was overwhelmed by the stories of selfless giving. They told of people, driven by the desire to ensure that their organs, or those of their loved ones, would be made available so someone else might live.

Because we view the body as God's creation, we hold it in high esteem. We use the term "sanctity of life" correctly. And for good reason. Humankind has the imprint of Christ: we are created in his image.

7

This calls us to seek every means available to alleviate suffering, enhance the quality of health, and extend life itself. There are many legitimate concerns which surface with the development of a new medical procedure. For example, we resist the taking of fetal tissue made available because of an abortion and using it for a transplant. The possibility of designer organs—in which a child is produced for the sake of a good tissue match—is troubling.

But that does not mean the transplant of organs from those who have died should not be used in a God-honoring way to assist the continuance of that which is God's gift: life itself. Neither does it prohibit loving acts of donating a living organ, as in the case of a kidney.

May the reading of this interesting and informative story, *Wings of Hope*, written by Henry Plett, be used to help us in a rapidly changing world of science and technology to know first the giver of life, so we may discern the legitimate limits of that life.

—*Brian C. Stiller*
  Executive Director, The Evangelical Fellowship of Canada, Editor in Chief, Faith Today *magazine*
  Coauthor, Lifegifts, *Stoddard, 1990.*

Special Thanks

To Dr. Ghent, Dr. Grant, and Dr. Wall, for their expertise, precision, and counsel during Roxanne's illness.

To Nettie, for the sacrificial way in which she gave of herself, her time, and her love in being there when needed. She went the limit as far as showing a mother's love and concern. Her diary formed the basis of this book.

To Ron and Eleanor, for the unselfish way they gave of themselves, their home, and their love to become more than parents to us during our stay in their home.

To John and Tina, for their sacrificial love and caring on short notice when we needed them.

To Jean, who became such a close friend and offered her home for us to use during their holiday. It helped fill a need in our family.

To the many members of the medical staff, who performed their tasks so well. They went beyond their call of duty in making our stay in London more pleasant.

To the many friends, who so willingly gave their various tokens of love.

To Terry, for his editorial help.

To all of you, a big thank you!

—Henry Plett

A Note from Roxanne

In January 1987 my family and I were thrust into the world of pain, tears, and frustration—the world of organ transplantation. We knew little about it, and so we received a crash course. The strain on our family was monumental. We received much-needed support from friends and acquaintances as they shared our pain and spent hours in prayer on our behalf. To these faithful I wish to say, You helped us through our time of hardship.

This book was not written to make you feel sorry for us, nor to relive the gory details, but rather to share with others the comfort we experienced. We feel that others need to know how God has answered prayer for us. I strongly believe that God performed a miracle in my life. Someday you too may have a need in a crisis experience. God will not let you down. You don't have to wait for a crisis. God is ready to step in right now.

This book was also written to help point out another need. There is a long list of people who need organs: kidneys, hearts, livers, and lungs as well as others on an ever-expanding list. The medical technology is there to provide the transplants, but the organs are not always available.

Should you be considering yourself as a potential donor? It may not be a pleasant thought, but it may be a gesture of life to someone in need, a gift of something you no longer have any use for. Through that gift another can have a second chance. Have you filled out a donor card? It would take only a moment to sign the back of your driver's license. Think about it.

—*Roxanne Plett*

1

The cool winter weather of December was upon us. In typical Calgary fashion, the temperature vacillated between the bitter cold of mid-November and the chinooks that came only days later. The glamour and glitter of Christmas was in the air and with it came the expectancy, festivity, and excitement so obvious at such a time of year in Alberta, Canada. It was on such a day that Roxanne calmly said to us, "I've made an appointment to see our family doctor." For her to make such a move on her own, we knew things must be serious.

Although my reaction was not one of immediate panic, I did have some concerns. In January of 1985, nearly two years earlier, Roxanne had developed some symptoms which had caused the doctors to take a second look. She was sixteen years old and in grade 10 when she had suddenly developed a severe pain in her joints which could be classified as typically rheumatoid. Teenagers should not have rheumatism or arthritis; it just isn't cool! Nor do they have time for such interferences in the routines of life.

Numerous tests became the order of the day. First there were visits to the family doctor, then to the specialist, then to other specialists. The results seemed to be pointing in one direction, the possibility of lupus. What a stroke of bad luck against an active teenager! She was told that such pain could be a part of regular life, and that dealing with it may include a lifelong pattern of drugs. It could, however, be kept under control, and life would be near normal.

Whatever it was, it was hard to accept. Severe pain in the joints was all too common. Swollen joints and fingers began to show in her performance. The piano, which had been an instrument of pleasure, now became an implement of near torture. Fingers could no longer move nimbly about as far and as quickly. Walking became a concerted effort, with each step becoming more painful. But there was sudden relief when a cold and sniffles took over. Strangely, the pain in the joints would vanish when she had a cold. What a strange phenomenon!

I gathered limited knowledge that lupus is not joint-related at all. Instead, it is a disease of an over-active immune system. Thus, when the body is healthy, the immune system searches throughout the body looking for things to attack in its role as a disease preventer. If no ailment is found, it begins to turn on itself and attack something close at hand. The joints seem a reasonable place to begin. However, it still has enough sense to remember its real function, to keep the body free from disease.

It has no problem identifying a cold as such an intruder, and wastes no time in mounting an attack. In the process, however, it leaves what it was doing and concentrates on the new enemy. With all the energy of the immune system directed in its proper direction, the pain in the joints suddenly disappears. Several times this situation surfaced with Roxanne. Relief in the joints seem to come whenever a cold or minor illness developed for the body to fight.

As a couple, Nettie and I had little time to even discuss the possibility of having a sick child in the household. Our life was busy, and illness simply was not that common in our home. We enjoyed our health immensely. We had always had a healthy family. Perhaps we were still of the old school, whose people spent little time with doctors in the firm belief that the body, with God's help, would look after itself. For Roxanne to see so many doctors in quick succession was a new experience.

Then, over a period of time, the pain went away. Perhaps it had only been a virus, we were told, something that had to run its course, and for which there was no treatment. Perhaps it was her diet or the medicine given in the early stages of diagnosis that had put the pain on hold. In retrospect, I see that it was the first of a series of signs which pointed out to us that health, and life itself, is fragile. We must learn to appreciate every moment available to us. We so often take it for granted.

On that December day, when the pain resurfaced, we were reminded again of the frailty of our health.

If one is not alert, the mind can play tricks and imagination can build on one's worst fears. Could it be that the disease was back again, and that the last months had simply been a time of remission? Or could it be that my daughter would be on a pain-controlling drug for the rest of her life to help her lead some form of subnormal life? Worse yet, could it be that my daughter would end up in a wheelchair with crippled joints and pain too severe to bear? Such illnesses are hardly acceptable for elderly people, let alone for teenagers.

Little did we know that what we were experiencing as a family, and the thoughts that were running rampant through my mind, were helping to set the stage for what lay ahead of us. God had a lot in store for us, and this was only a beginning. Much more would be sent our way, but God would only give us a little at a time.

According to 1 Corinthians 10:13, God would stand right there with us in order to give us strength for the task. It's good that we didn't know what the future held. It would simply have overwhelmed us if we had known what was coming.

2

Events began to develop in rapid succession. Many times in the next few weeks, we would hardly have time to sit down and wonder what was due to happen next, before it actually did occur.

Christmas came with its festivities and we enjoyed being together as a family. Our oldest son, Nelson, and our daughter-in-law of one year, Shelly, were there. Lyndon came home from Hepburn, Saskatchewan, where he was attending school at Bethany Bible Institute. He brought a special friend with him, and this was to be a time of getting to know her as well. Corinne and Gwen, in their early-teen and preteen years, were there with the innocence of their desire to see that the gifts and the festivities were experienced to the utmost. That made up our family. With eight people around the table or sharing together in games and laughter, the season promised to be full of enjoyment.

Or could it be? Every glance in the direction of Roxanne was a vivid reminder that things were not all well. For the moment, she could laugh with us, but loss of appetite, pain, and discomfort were beginning to tell a tale. How could she wait till the latter part of January for her scheduled visit to the specialist? What should she do in the meantime?

Frustrating experiences have a way of piling up from time to time. This holiday season was no exception. As a schoolteacher, I had a "job jar," holding quite a significant number of notes on projects to do during the holidays, when I would have time. But in addition to these tasks, a series of new emergencies appeared. The transmission on the pickup truck suddenly needed attention. This would take both time and money. Next was the clothes drier, which I had repaired so many times before and attempted to fix once more. The stove quit working, the door needed fixing, and so it went, on and on. Anyone with an ear to the ground would have thought that the house was due to crumble.

But the spiritual ear can perceive even more if it is attentive to its surroundings. In retrospect, it seemed that we were getting a lesson on *important* things in life, things that had lasting value. Not things like the clothes drier, which after its latest repair, would have to be replaced entirely in early January. Maybe God was trying to tell us something about our material values. We were comfortable and had a lot of the amenities and conveniences of a nice home. Perhaps we needed a little *prying loose* from these material things.

Material things were not all. We needed a lesson in relationships as well. As mentioned previously,

Lyndon brought home a special friend with the intention of having us get to know her better. She had been at our home several times before and had won a warm spot in our hearts. It wasn't hard. She had a personality that quickly created a warm spot. What a shock when in the aftermath of the Christmas celebration, she called a time-out to go home and rethink the relationship. It was hard to see her go. But the experience would serve us well in the months to come, as we wrestled with, and reevaluated, things that were dear to us.

God still wasn't finished with us. Another lesson we needed to learn was the value and frailty of life. For years in my childhood and adolescent period, my family was not faced with death. Then in the space of a few months in 1972 we stood at graveside three times. Mary Ann, my sister-in-law, was a kidnap-murder victim; my dad was a victim of cancer; and my mother, the victim of a stroke. This is quite a shock to absorb, particularly in such a short period of time.

But we believe in God, who through Christ overcomes death and gives eternal life now and in the resurrection. We believe in heaven and hell. We believe that persons who have committed their lives to God can count on life in heaven. Others who have made this commitment will follow later and thus look forward to a family reunion some day. The circle can be unbroken. What a comfort to know that someday we will see our loved ones again.

Death stalked our family again in 1978. Life had resumed its seminormal pace and Jake, my brother, had remarried after Mary Ann's death. Marion, his new wife, became the instant mother of his two boys, Nelson and Lyndon, as they resided in Edmonton. They were blessed with two girls, Carlene and Christine, as well. As Jake analyzed the agony which he and his family had gone through in seven months of uncertainty, bitterness, and waiting, he was encouraged to write of his experiences. In 1976 his book, *Valley of Shadows,* was published in paperback form.

Promotion of a book is essential, and suddenly Jake found himself touring Canada on speaking engagements, sharing his experiences in churches in various provinces. One of these speaking engagements took him to Cranbrook to speak at a women's banquet. It was agreed that Marion would accompany him on this trip. It was a blustery day in February when PWA flight 314 attempted to avoid a snowplow clearing the runway at Cranbrook. The pilot was unable to make the necessary adjustments and crashed in a ball of flame nearby. Forty-one of the forty-seven persons on board were killed. Jake and Marion were among them.

Over the next days and weeks the closeness and the grimness of death became quite real. To bury a member of the family due to disease is one thing. But to bury two members at the same time, in the prime of life, is quite another. Four children had been left behind. Nettie and I found ourselves thrust into the midst of funeral arrangements, comforting the children, planning for the future of the family, assessing the will, and looking after legal matters.

Marion's brother Art and I were requested to fly to Cranbrook to identify the bodies—certainly a gruesome assignment. Furthermore, my name, along with Marilyn's, showed up in the will as guardians. Marilyn was Marion's identical twin sister and was very close to her. Plans for a changing lifestyle with larger families was a real possibility. Should their family be split up? Should all children be kept together? How large can a family be in today's society and still be economically viable? We had three children of our own; to add four would make seven. Lloyd and Marilyn had two children, and four more would make six. Possible? Yes, but definitely crowded.

Before long we were considering the possibility of a divided family, as the split could be quite natural. Nelson and Lyndon were from a previous marriage and were of closer blood relationship to our family than to Lloyd and Marilyn's. On the other hand, Carlene and Christine were just as close in relationship to Lloyd and Marilyn as to us.

When we left Edmonton, and the tears and dust had settled somewhat, our family had grown by two. Nelson and Lyndon had become members of our family. Carlene and Christine had become members of Lloyd and Marilyn's family. To say that adjustments to such a change were hard would be an understatement. We had three girls. Now two boys were added. We had three members of the family under ten years of age. Now two teenagers were being added. What a *growing experience*!

We had another reminder of death later that same

21

year. In a routine medical checkup for my class 2 driver's license, the doctor found a growth in my chest cavity, near my heart. Concern was obvious. If it was malignant, then my time would be short. While I waited for surgery, there was great fear and anxiety. What if? Would Nettie be left as a widow, now that we had five children? It was during this wait for a hospital bed that Pete passed away. He was a fine Christian friend who had suffered from a heart condition for some time. Again, a young man was taken in his prime. What did God have in store for me? The reminders were coming quickly.

In early October, I was invited to book into Foothills Hospital for surgery. I found it difficult to express my feelings. The doctors were positive, but because of the rapid growth of the tumor, they had cause for concern. No doubt the calmness that pervaded our feelings was due to God's presence with us.

The operation was a success. There was no malignancy, and I had a rare phenomenon called a dermoid tumor. It had every form of tissue in it that is a part of the human body. The body does some strange things. Possibly the fertilized egg split and one portion of it lay dormant all these years, while I, the other half of the egg, grew up. Now something, possibly the hardships we had experienced earlier, had triggered this form of growth. Perhaps it was my attempt at giving birth to my twin. You can tell that my mother instincts are not very good!

Now in December of 1986 we received another reminder. John was a good friend of ours who had suffered from a heart condition for some time. After a severe heart attack some years earlier, he had adjusted his lifestyle out of consideration for his weak heart. As I visited with him, we shared together some of the goals and aspirations we had. He openly talked of how his hopes could be jeopardized because of his health.

As we prayed together before I left, I felt he was committing his future into the Lord's hands and entrusting God with the outcome. Only weeks later, he passed away. Another reminder was being sent our way that time was a gift, and life in its fleeting moments needed to be utilized.

But I was still unaware that many lessons on the frailty of life were still untaught. It is good that such learnings come a little at a time, lest we become overwhelmed by a flood if they all come at once.

3

The new year started relatively quiet with little fanfare by our family. As usual we simply committed the future into God's hands and felt with confidence that he would lead the way. But would we be willing to follow? Would we understand the direction that God led, or the rugged terrain over which he would shepherd us? Leading was God's responsibility; following was ours.

Teenagers are not meant to be sissies. As weak as she was, Roxanne talked of going skiing. Her condition deteriorated steadily over the next few weeks. She still refused to give up. School was not to be taken lightly, and she continued to attend classes in spite of her misery. Sometimes her work was done with her head resting on her desk. She developed a fever that refused to subside.

On January 9, Roxanne made her next doctor's visit. It was to her physician, Dr. Addison. Walking had become a problem and there was severe pain in her joints. On the morning of her appointment the first signs of jaundice appeared and she pointed this out to me. The diagnosis was a general one, pointing to the possibility of a stomach infection, but with the warnings of a need to check out a malfunctioning liver. Over the weekend, her color became more jaundiced. On Monday Dr. Addison needed only one look to convince himself that the next step was admittance to Foothills Hospital, here in Calgary.

As parents, we continued to be totally unsuspecting. Children often have mild illnesses. Sometimes they become seriously ill and require hospitalization. But it is only a matter of time before they are healthy and on the run again. Why should Roxanne be any different? Did she not have a healthy track record? Even when the word *hepatitis* was mentioned in conjunction with her color, we thought even this was a minor technicality. There was still room for us to learn.

Room 632 was a ward with four beds. Sharing facilities is no problem, I thought. She won't be here long. But the fever continued to hold at 104 degrees. How long can a person maintain such high temperatures? The color deepened. Confusion showed its first signs in her. Conversations began to be repetitive, and Roxanne's memory seemed to be failing.

The doctors talked frequently of liver failure, but continued to be positive. "The liver can rebuild itself," they said. "It isn't like the heart, which develops scar tissue which cannot be replaced."

All we needed now was the ability of the body to withstand the disease which was causing the problem and allow the liver to begin the process of rebuilding. The diagnosis was still uncertain. Hepatitis was almost a certainty because of the color. But additional complications were present. Doctors and specialists began to speak of a combination of infectious hepatitis and mononucleosis. Later the diagnosis was changed to viral hepatitis. The source was unknown.

No, Roxanne was not a junkie on dirty needles in some back-street hovel, nor was she picking it up off the street. That simply was not her lifestyle. Yet the disease was there and was running its course. In the race against time, which would be stronger: the disease, or the rehabilitative power of the body? If time was on her side the body might indeed heal itself. If not . . . one could only imagine the worst.

By January 14, there were periodic but distinct signs of confusion. "The poisons," they explained, "are not being processed and flushed out of the system by the liver. The brain is being affected by these toxins and clear thoughts are not always possible. The body desperately attempts to clear itself of the toxins, but because it cannot do so through the normal channels, the last effort is expulsion through the skin. It is a good thought, but slow and inefficient. The skin is *inexperienced* in this process and begins to turn yellow from the poisons."

Roxanne began to retain fluid and her body showed signs of swelling. Her stomach was hard and swollen.

The theoretical explanation was good, but it did little to take away the hurt of seeing a body pretending it was a chameleon in autumn! Or of hearing the

26

confusion of her fragmented speech. Although we believed Roxanne was showing signs of improvement, these two telltale signs were a constant reminder that all was not well.

Liver failure was still the diagnosis, and now a new term entered our vocabulary for the first time. The word was *transplant*. It was mentioned for the first time on January 14. Nettie and I didn't even discuss it as a possibility. It was so remote that it hardly deserved our attention. Surely, all we needed was to give her liver time to stabilize itself and then begin the process of recuperation and rebuilding. But it didn't happen.

On Sunday, the possibility of transplant was mentioned twice in brief discussion with medical staff. This time Nettie and I began to discuss it as a possibility. Still, it was something that people did elsewhere, in South Africa, in Pittsburgh, in Loma Linda, but not here. Although we discussed it, we still did not believe in the reality of it.

The staff at my school was concerned. So was Marv, my principal. On Monday morning, during a lull in my timetable, I spent some time in his office. We discussed the possibilities of a transplant and the need for members of the family to be available to such a patient. Marv is an understanding person. He made it clear that if such a problem arose, I was to drop my responsibilities at school and be with my family, whether that meant here, or in London, Ontario.

We talked about provisions made by the school board in such eventualities. He confirmed that in such circumstances the staff would be more than willing to stand by with any support that might be needed in my classroom or administrative tasks. Before I left his office that morning, I assured him that this type of thing happens elsewhere, but not in Calgary, and not to the Plett family. I would not have to leave my post. By now you may consider me a slow learner!

That afternoon there was a call for me. It was Dr. Hershfield, the specialist who was looking after Roxanne. His voice was tense.

"We have come to the end of our ability here in Calgary, and we see the only possibility of help is a liver transplant. We have already been in contact with doctors in London and we suggest that you plan to go as quickly as possible."

"How much time do I have to make up my mind?" I asked.

"You should be there within forty-eight hours" was the reply.

Forty-eight hours! But what about my job? What about my family? What about arrangements? How do we get there? Where should we stay? Where does the money come from?

For a moment, I put my head on my desk as I let the message sink in. Then I prayed for guidance as I choked back the tears. We would need a lot. This time reality was too harsh. This was indeed abrupt.

Within minutes I had received Marv's complete support to simply look after needs in my family. He would make arrangements at the school. Last-minute instructions were hard to give while I was choking back the tears. But the people were so understanding.

I was out the door and on my way to the hospital, floating as if in a make-believe world. Certainly there would still be a turn of events. Had we not prayed for healing? Where was God now when we needed him so desperately? Was the process of his healing touch going to include a trip to London, a city where I knew no one? It certainly did not have to. He could heal Roxanne even now before she left. Would God do it?

Nettie was running errands that afternoon and had not been a part of the discussion. We met in the hospital parking lot and had but a few brief moments to discuss the possibilities that lay before us. Roxanne lay in her bed, totally oblivious to the commotion about her. In the time it took me to get to the hospital, events began to occur rapidly.

The forty-eight hours of which Dr. Hershfield spoke on the phone had suddenly shrunk to *overnight*. A bed was waiting for her in University Hospital in London. The air ambulance crew had been contacted. They would come, assess Roxanne's condition, and see what was needed for the flight in terms of personnel, medications, care, and equipment. We were to fly out as soon as possible, perhaps even on the ambulance with her. At least it was a momentary comfort, to be with her while we traveled. But even that was not to be.

When the ambulance attendant arrived, he assessed her condition as being critical. He made arrangements to take extra personnel as well as extra equipment. They would leave at 7:30 a.m. Tickets would be provided for us to follow on a commercial airline as soon as possible. But what about other arrangements?

Contacts had to be made. Where would Corinne and Gwen stay in our absence? We had to plan for their care. We needed support, with our spirits so low and our nerves so frayed. Decisions made under those circumstances might not be seen as totally valid later. We needed some counsel to keep us making logical decisions.

During such times people turn unashamedly to their spiritual leaders. Thus, I phoned Pastor Brad with the basic details. Before long the church prayer chain was activated, and people began to pray throughout the city. Also, before long, the moral support we needed was there with us at the hospital. Pastor Henry and Vi came, as well as numerous church elders. They had gathered to pray with us and for us.

A phone call to the school was in order; the teachers were colleagues, but they were also concerned friends. I called to say that plans were for us to be in London by Tuesday. Marv had called the staff together right after school and shared with them the update on the news about our family. Little did I know that there was purpose even in that.

Mark was a teacher on my staff. As colleagues we enjoyed and encouraged each other in our teaching endeavors. He was from London and had moved to Calgary several years previously to begin teaching. There was no question in his mind that our trip to

London and his parents living in London were more than a mere coincidence. He immediately made a call to his mother and mentioned our need for accommodations in London. Would the Hunniford home be open to such a remote need? When he suggested it to me on the phone, I was overwhelmed.

We hadn't even had time to think in terms of preparations in Calgary, let alone arrangements in London. Needless to say, I accepted at once. What a relief, to think that one more detail had already been looked after. The Hunnifords' approval of our coming was an answer to prayer: in Isaiah 65:24 the Lord says, "Before they call I will answer." If they had known the time frame to which they were being committed, they might have hesitated. It's sometimes good that we function only one day at a time.

Things were not happening merely according to circumstance. There was more to it than that. How was it that my sister Tina and her husband, John, had become available to look after our family? John had retired in the previous September from his role as a principal with the Calgary Board of Education. It had not been planned that way but suddenly, near the end of the previous school year, pressures made such a decision seem wise. Their prayer had been that God would make them available for whatever purpose he had in mind.

Their willingness to accept the responsibilities of taking care of Corinne and Gwen made leaving home much easier. No one knew how long we would be gone. How could we travel to another city, leaving two young members of the family to fend for themselves, along with the adjustments and hurts that they too were experiencing?

The answer was obvious. John and Tina would move into our house for an indefinite period and look after the girls. That way there would be no need for them to change schools or drive distances to their school. And at least the home would have a measure of constancy for them in the turmoil that they were going through.

Little did these new parents realize that they were committing themselves for a long period of time. Perhaps it was a good thing they didn't know, or they might have had second thoughts. They were so gracious in their support.

We gathered as a family in the hospital waiting room. All of us were shocked at the rapidity with which things were occurring. Nelson and Shelly had just returned from a post-Christmas visit to Shelly's parents in Ontario. My welcome-back message to my son was the news that it was our turn to go to Ontario, but under much more duress than they had experienced. Lyndon was back in Bethany and we gave the news to him via telephone.

How does one share such an intimate moment? There was little that could be said. The tears and hugs in the waiting room, the pauses in the telephone conversations, and the concern of the medical staff told the whole story. Roxanne was in critical condition.

We needed to rely on each other, as the strain could become unbearable. We were headed into the unknown, and we were comforted only by caring friends and our faith in a God who knows the future and leads us one step at a time. Nettie and I would be with Roxanne through her experiences, but the family would be far away. Distance has a way of making the pain even harsher.

Meanwhile, Roxanne's confusion continued. She sat up in bed, ate some food, and talked with us, assuring us that she knew who we were, where she was, where she was going, and what lay ahead for her. But later she remembered none of it. She began to get restless and frustrated with the discomfort of the IV (intravenous) lines. For us, her reaction was perhaps harder to accept than the pain that she was experiencing.

All of us had a lot to learn in the weeks that lay ahead. In such a condition we cleaned up her room and left the hospital. Early tomorrow the ambulance would transport her to the airport, where a Lear jet would fly her to London for a liver transplant. Can you imagine our feelings? We needed *wings of hope*.

4

How does one prepare for a trip with so little knowledge of what may happen, and no outline as to time, location, or activity? Wildest imagination begins to serve as a guide. And how does one pack in a few hours for a trip like this? Mechanically, and with a heavy heart, we set out to gather the few belongings that we would need.

Our flight tickets had been purchased and arranged for by Ken, the ambulance attendant, so at least we need not concern ourselves with that detail. Alberta Health Care would look after the travel cost. There wasn't much organization to our activity that evening as we scurried about, making phone calls to family members, packing, giving instructions, spending time with Pastor Brad, packing some more, and discussing more possibilities and *what ifs* in a never-ending circle.

With our flight time at noon on Tuesday, we felt that many of our friends and family should be contacted personally. But under such pressure, the time moves by far too quickly, and we found ourselves on the aircraft, alone with our thoughts and without our family members.

Our concerns were obvious. How would Roxanne do on the trip? Would the doctors in London be able to help her? Would they be able to help her without a transplant? How would the Hunnifords react to our presence in their home? How would the family handle the whole situation? Would they agree with the concept of a transplant?

The plane was delayed and we were able to ponder these thoughts even longer. Our anxiety over our sick daughter was not improved by the wait, particularly since a transfer was to be made from Toronto to London. A delay put that connection in jeopardy. The word we had to learn over and over again was *patience,* in more connotations than one!

Even the longest and slowest hours pass eventually, and we found ourselves touching down in London, a city that had just had a major blizzard. Nothing moves rapidly enough when you are rushing to a bedside, let alone through snow-clogged streets. The cab dropped us off at the hospital at about 9:00 p.m., and we were introduced to our new surroundings.

There it was, with its commotion, public-address calls, hospital smells, and noises. University Hospital was known as a transplant center, so where was this famous transplant unit? We were directed to the spot and approached it with misgivings. Such a small area, with only four beds, and, yes, there was Roxanne. She was awake and somewhat coherent as she talked of where she was and why she was there.

Although we thought she comprehended the situation, she recalled none of this discussion later. Her memory of the ambulance trip was limited to short periods of noise, vibrations, and cold. If God was going to heal her, he would have to move quickly. Her body simply was not doing what it was expected to do.

It is not pleasant to cope with traveling to a strange place while the uncertainty of the future lies heavily on one. Nor does it help to arrive in completely unfamiliar surroundings. But greater still is the concern when heavy uncertainty remains because of lack of knowledge or acting in ignorance.

We knew nothing of transplants. These were things that happened, but they happened elsewhere. The news media had been of no help in this regard. The only transplants we had heard about were body parts placed into patients who had struggled through their illness and passed away quietly. They had made their contribution to the advances of technology and science. We knew of no recipient of a transplant who had survived a number of years, or who were leading a normal or seminormal posttransplant life.

There was nothing in our sphere of knowledge which could lend a comforting thought. So where should we turn for our comfort? The source was obvious: Go to God's Word. Turn to the comforts which God himself promised at a time of distress. The Bible is full of promises and it seems as though times of distress bring out such passages.

Isaiah 43:1-2 is one such passage: "But now thus says the Lord, he who created you, O Jacob, he who formed you, O Israel: 'Fear not, for I have redeemed you; I have called you by name, you are mine. When you pass through the waters I will be with you; and through the rivers, they shall not overwhelm you; when you walk through fire you shall not be burned, and the flame shall not consume you.' "

What we needed was to build up our confidence in the possibility of a successful transplant. Where were the positive examples of the acclaimed University Hospital and their success? These encouraging exhibits were not long in coming.

The multiple-organ-transplant unit (MOTS), where Roxanne was placed, was made up of four beds with facilities that were of near-intensive-care caliber treatment. The transplant patient after surgery went from the intensive care unit (ICU) into the MOTS unit and then eventually onto the main ward to join other patients. On our arrival in her room we found our first live and vibrant example of transplant success.

In the bed next to Roxanne was Lyndon, with a heart transplant of only three days. He was sitting up in bed, talking, and eating Jello. Heart-transplant patients, in my estimation, simply could not function that way, let alone in three days. Perhaps this was indeed a hospital in which miracles occurred. The following day, we saw others. Lois, with a liver transplant of only ten days, was still on IV. Yet she was happy, talkative, courageous, and encouraging, along with many other descriptive words not yet in our vocabulary of transplant terminology.

Those two live examples were probably the best therapy which we could have had in the early days of our stay in London. It boosted our faith that medicine and science had come a long way. With excellent medical care in conjunction with the healing and soothing power of God, we could, indeed, expect a miracle in Roxanne's life. We counted on a show of teamwork between God and the doctors to produce a miracle.

We received assurances from the nurses and a phone call from Steve Turner, a social worker whose duty was to look after the needs of liver-transplant patients and their families. Some of the darkness and heaviness of unfamiliar surroundings lifted ever so slightly. It was 9:30 p.m. and we had one more thing to do that night. We still had not met the Hunnifords. On landing at the airport, while waiting for a cab, we had called to make arrangements for Ron and Eleanor to pick us up at the hospital at 9:30.

They were waiting for us in the lobby. The initial greetings of several unfamiliar people suddenly vanished into the background as we felt their warmth and acceptance. In retrospect, it seemed almost as if we had always known them. Their home was opened and their facilities made available to us. We were given a quaint little room downstairs, which more than adequately served our purpose.

But that wasn't all. A closeness quickly developed in which we sensed that they and their family gave of themselves, their love, and concern as much as their home. It was a friendship that was born and bonded in turmoil, and we soon sensed that it would be a strong bond. Is it any wonder that they became like parents to us? If they had known that this was to be home for us and a portion of our family for so long, would their reaction have been any different?

Wednesday was a busy day. Just being around a hospital does not sound like much of a career. But repeatedly we were unable to find time to do all the necessary and important things. We were there by 11:00 a.m. to talk to Steve, the social worker. His responsibility was to make us feel comfortable with the transition of moving to London and to deal with the things that lay ahead. And what a job he did! He gave medical information about the liver, and the statistics on the success and failure of transplants at University Hospital. Then he helped us meet and interact with actual transplant patients to see for ourselves how well they were doing. Also on the list of things to show us was the painful tour through the ICU.

"This is what your daughter will look like when she comes out of the OR (operating room)," he explained. "She will have all these lines, some for feeding, some for medications, some for life support. Don't be afraid of all the equipment."

How could we not be afraid? The noise was unbearable. Equipment beeped and hissed and grunted as it followed its precise instructions. Lines crisscrossed in so many directions that, to us, it seemed even the medications would get lost in the process. Patients lay there motionless and pale, perhaps barely alive, as nurses, doctors, and technicians scurried about doing their tasks and monitoring their vitals.

We thought: Today we see a patient lying there, but that is all she is to us. Next week that still form will be that of our daughter. How will the lines and equipment and noise and activity affect us then? That would indeed be a harsh reality.

I tried to imagine that the patient was Roxanne, but it was impossible. My daughter should not even be in the hospital, much less in the ICU in London. For the moment I put the picture out of my mind. Maybe she will still get better, I thought. Was it a vain hope? Or was it a deep-rooted faith in a God who had proven himself to us so many times before, and was now standing by and hoping to reveal the same to us again?

But the doctors' diagnosis was the same: "Acute liver failure. She needs a liver fast. She is fading. We have put her on a code 1. Perhaps a liver will become available soon!"

5

Going into this experience, our medical knowledge was minimal or nonexistent. Now we began to receive facts in large quantities. For someone who didn't recognize the value and function of a liver before, this was indeed overwhelming.

A liver performs about 5000 functions. It serves as a chemical filter for the blood, breaking down and getting rid of toxins that can poison the body. It produces bile, a digestive aid which helps to break down foods into substances usable by the body through metabolism. The storage of nutrients, sugars, and vitamins takes place here as well. Blood-clotting agents, such as heparin, are stored here. In addition, it plays a major role in the maintenance of body temperature. Numerous other functions are performed here as well. Not bad for a single organ!

Each organ is wonderful in its own way. A liver can rebuild itself with new tissue over time, a process which the heart cannot do. But the heart is easier to replace because it has only a single function. A mechanical heart is a possibility because of that singular task, but no one has been able to reproduce all the functions of a liver. It is simply too complicated.

There are two kidneys, so if one suddenly malfunctions, it is possible for a body to thrive with only one. Some organs are not needed. For example, a gall bladder can be removed without serious consequences. Not so with the liver. Truly, we are "fearfully and wonderfully made" (Psalm 139:13-16, KJV).

In order to transplant the liver, several things must be taken into consideration. One is the time available to the patient. Roxanne was in dire straits and had to have an organ within a few days. This limited the amount of time that could be spent looking for a suitable donor.

Another consideration is the size of the recipient. Roxanne was only a teenager, and not a big one at that, weighing in at 115 pounds. Her donor could not be large. Perhaps it would have to be a teenager as well, or perhaps a small woman.

Then, blood type is extremely important. To be compatible, the donor and the recipient must have the same blood type. Roxanne had type *B*, which is not one of the more common types.

In summarizing her chances of survival to us on our first visit with him, Dr. Ghent did not give us a rosy picture. Her size and blood type were problems, and her condition was quickly deteriorating. His estimate was only a 30 percent chance of survival. But the organ must be found first. Without a donor, there would be no transplant; and without a transplant, there was no hope at all.

But doctors have a way of being reassuring, even if they have to be brutally honest at times. He talked of the success rate of the transplant program at University Hospital and how successful it had become since the present team of Dr. Grant, Dr. Wall, and Dr. Ghent began working together. With the appearance of cyclosporine on the medical list of anti-rejection drugs, the percentages had increased dramatically.

Roxanne had another thing in her favor. Her kidneys were functioning well, and if that system would continue to hold out, her chances of waiting longer for a donor were much better. Suddenly, the 85 percent success rate of which he spoke did not seem totally unrealistic. We had hundreds of people praying for her as well. Together, we could witness a miracle.

There was a slight improvement in Roxanne's condition when we spent time with her on Wednesday. Although not everything she said was coherent, it was more encouraging than it had been the previous night. On occasion, she would ask Nettie to fix her jacket so she would not be so cold. At this time she had been hospitalized for nearly two weeks and had no need for her jacket.

Alongside the jumble in her thinking was some clarity about her surroundings. She knew where she was. She had better know; she was asked that question dozens of times a day. Now she remembered her family back home, wondering how they were, and who was looking after them.

However, she still failed to recognize the real reason for being in London. In Calgary we had repeatedly told her that her stay in London was for a transplant, but she had not comprehended it. So the explanation was given again, and repeated several times before the actual operation. Now a new problem began to surface. She was afraid for what lay ahead. I don't believe she can be faulted for that.

Personnel and programs need to be in place and cooperating to make transplant patients and their families as comfortable as possible under the circumstances. Such things happened in London. Perhaps more than they realized, people helped to ease the burden under which we struggled. One of these persons was Steve, who has already been mentioned. He ministered to us through his openness regarding our concerns, Roxanne's needs, and the severity of the situation. He shared knowledge of the procedures, listened to our fears, and capably answered our questions.

Physical needs were also important. We needed a car for transportation. Eleanor had lent us her car for the first day while she traveled by transit bus. This was not acceptable to us on a continuing basis, and we looked for a rental car. When Host Rent a Car found that we were family members of a transplant patient, the manager instantly offered us a $100 deduction on the monthly rate. Although money is not the greatest factor when life is at stake, the gesture was welcome and greatly appreciated, regardless of how small or simple it may seem. People who give at such times may never know how much that help can mean.

On the hill overlooking the hospital was the "Mount." It was a girls' school that had been transformed into temporary lodging for families of transplant patients. Although we personally never had the occasion to experience its warmth, the reports we heard from others were quite positive and showed again that family needs had been taken into consideration. It became more than a home away from home. It was also a place where people with common concerns could share with others.

One of the most important built-in factors not organized by the hospital was the strength received from families of other transplant patients. Vickie was one such person. She met us shortly after we got there and helped us to feel at home in our new surroundings. Her husband, Bob, had received his second liver a few days earlier, but had developed complications and was still in a coma. Over the next few days, we took turns supporting each other.

Churches were there to help as well, so we made contact with Komoka Community Church, a sister congregation to Dalhousie Community Church, which we attended in Calgary. We knew no one in the congregation and were simply reaching out in desperation for someone to be a friend to us and to lend us emotional support.

How would a church respond to a new family with such a need and asking so boldly for help? Is it an accepted fact that transplants are a part of God's plan? If so, how does one pray for a donor? As a couple, we had not had time to ponder the ethics of this problem for ourselves. Maybe the people would not even be willing to become involved in prayer support.

But, one by one, the members we contacted responded beautifully. Komoka Church had a young pastor by the name of Gordon Russell. Our call to the church was on one of his first days in the office. What a way to begin his new pastorate! We asked for their prayer as a church and for his visits to the hospital for Roxanne's sake.

Pastor Gordon came on Friday, but it was not a good day for her. She had slipped into a coma and her response to us was minimal. Occasionally she would open her eyes and look around briefly. When the pastor introduced himself to us and then came in to pray with her, I'm convinced he had some mixed feelings. Roxanne at this point did not show any awareness.

In attempting to reach out to friends and familiar faces, we began to make contacts with friends from college days. We knew few others in Ontario. Our next telephone conversation was with John, in St. Catharines. John and Betty were personal friends of ours during college years. Our times together had included carefree days of single life in the dorms, with all their nonchalance and camaraderie.

After marriage, our ways parted and they, having tried their hand at several careers, had felt the call of God into pastoral work. After several years in seminary, they were back in Ontario with the Scott Street Church. It was good to renew old acquaintances, but not under such circumstances. Their response was great: "When can we come and see you?" To be in Ontario together seemed wonderful, but we were still two hours apart.

Over the next few days we contacted John and Margaret Wiebe, Shelly's parents. Sharing children is a good way to get to know people, and before long our brief earlier acquaintance had developed into a much deeper friendship based on the love and care which they showered on us. Over the next few months, they participated deeply in our experiences.

Rainer and Ann Wohlgemut were also personal friends from college times. They lived in Kitchener, an hour's drive away, and over the next months traveled the road to London many times to see us and to share our experiences. They had teenagers as well, and Peter's visits with Roxanne were times when *teen talk* could be utilized.

John and Carol Hiebert were likewise college friends. They had made their home on a small orchard farm in Virgil. We had stayed at their home at the time of Nelson and Shelly's wedding. Their responses to our needs were also overwhelming.

Friendships in the Komoka Church developed quickly. They were most supportive in every respect. They took us into their lives and into their prayers. Barney and Diane McCann were one couple who became close friends with us. The regularity of their visits, the times we spent in their home, and the evenings they took us out for supper, were indeed overwhelming. Their two teenage girls helped to lift Roxanne's spirits many times. Their friendship went beyond the call of duty and will last for years to come.

Each of these friends not only responded to us, but they also updated the prayer chains in their churches praying for Roxanne's health. The support was a tremendous blessing from God.

A patient takes on different hues when ill, but there are limits to what at least seems relatively normal. With partial kidney failure, as well as liver failure, Roxanne's color deepened to a dark yellow. Luckily the bedsheets were varying shades of blue and green, or she might have been lost in the colors! My hand or Nettie's hand holding hers provided a sharp contrast in pinks and yellows. Her tears left stains on the pillow. As her systems failed, her color deepened.

She slipped deeper into a coma, and another concern gripped us. Her body was no longer able to get rid of its fluids, and her size and weight were becoming unbelievable. Her frail body, which before was so small, now was huge. As parents, our task was to be there and to provide her with whatever she needed, regardless of her unbecoming state. Such minor things dare not interfere.

Although she did not respond to us any longer, the medical staff encouraged us to be at her side, and to talk to her as much as possible. How large is your repertoire of things to talk about when you do all the talking? Mine is not large and I found myself quoting Scripture to her, reciting and even singing songs to her, praying with her, and assuring her of our love. She appeared oblivious and made no response, but we felt the encouragement was essential. What if she was semiconscious and needed moral support in the form of hearing our voice, feeling the touch of a hand, or the assurance of our love, as we sat by?

It was during this time that I became aware of a shortcoming I had. How many Scripture passages does one know? How many verses to songs can one give from memory? I assure you that after several days at a bedside, you will use up your repertoire, as I did.

The diagnosis continued to be the same. "Roxanne is experiencing severe liver failure and must have an organ fast." The body could only hold its own for so long before failure of other systems would begin to occur. Her condition deteriorated as the kidneys started to show signs of failure. Her body temperature was extremely high, her blood pressure and pulse rate were high, and her breathing became rapid and labored. At this point the doctors made a decision. If they had to, they would give her an incompatible liver to prolong her life.

Roxanne had been on a code 1 on the organ donor list. This meant that she would be given a liver transplant when an organ became available. However, liver-transplant recipients have waited months until a suitable organ was found. By the doctors' expert analysis, her time was limited to several hours. With time constraints like that, one is sometimes compelled to take second best. The doctors were forced into such a decision.

There were several aspects which had to be considered. On a revised list of needed organs she was given a code 0, which means that an organ is needed desperately. Less needy patients must wait. Furthermore, because of the limited time available, exceptions would be made.

It was decided that the retrieval team would travel anywhere in North America to pick up an organ. Four hours of flying time from London was seen as the usual limit. A liver cannot be retrieved and stored indefinitely, but they were willing to go somewhat beyond the four-hour radius. In practical terms, this included an arc reaching as far as Calgary or beyond in Canada, and the Western, Midwestern, and Southern United States. A Lear jet makes this seem like a simple task.

An incompatible liver transplant poses a much greater chance of rejection, but this was another risk which the medical staff was willing to take. The operation would be used to buy time. Roxanne's condition simply did not allow the medical staff to wait for compatibility. Incompatibility could be countered with heavier doses of drugs, and other experimental treatments which we would see later. For the moment, time was the prime factor. While the medical staff worked, we prayed that her hours would somehow be extended.

With the decision made, things moved rapidly. As we learned later, Michael Bloch was promptly on the phone to hospitals around North America. The computer was updated with Roxanne's vital needs and constantly checked for a possible donor. Roxanne was moved to intensive care, where life-support systems could be attached. Her breathing was so labored that a respirator was necessary. More lines were attached for feeding, medication, and preparation for the transplant. Now the big question kept repeating itself in our minds. Would an organ become available?

Michael Bloch was the transplant coordinator, in charge of locating and looking after the retrieval of the organs needed for transplants at University Hospital. To aid him, an electronic network was in place, allowing hospitals across the continent to see at an instant what type of organs were needed. In some areas the call letters for arranging for organ transplants spell HOPE. It certainly took hope to keep us going.

Prospective transplant recipients were analyzed and placed on a code of importance. Code labels have been changed since then, but the categories at that time were as follows:

A code 3 person might need an organ but could live a fairly normal life until such an organ was found, at which time the operation would be performed. A wait of several months was possible.

A code 2 individual would probably still be an outpatient, but with a fairly advanced disorder and with more urgency and need. Each would likely wear a beeper and would live a seminormal life near the hospital until the day when the beeper would summon them to the hospital. They would admit themselves, and the transplant would be done on schedule. Still, it might be necessary to wait several weeks for an organ.

A code 1 patient would be hospitalized with an even greater urgency, and the computer would be scanned in greater detail based on the specific need. Urgency would show a preference for a code 1 over a code 3.

Code 0 was a crucial classification. An organ was needed and it was needed immediately. In the professional opinion of the doctors, time would be the major concern in acting in this category. If time was running out, a code 0 patient would get the organ that a code 3 person had time to wait for. Roxanne was a code 0, and it was Michael's job to get her a liver as quickly as possible.

It was late evening on January 24 when the decision was made to go anywhere in North America for even an incompatible liver for Roxanne. She was failing fast, and the diagnosis mentioned that she had only a few hours left to live.

The transplant team had finished another surgery by 5:00 p.m. that day. By 11:00 p.m. Mr. Bloch was back on the job after only a few hours at home. He worked around the clock, scanning the network, contacting hospitals to remind them of the urgency. By his estimation over 150 phone calls had to be made.

Suddenly, an organ became available in Colorado, roughly the right size, but not the right blood type. The medical staff decided it was time to act.

Now began the detailed task of bringing people, rooms, equipment, technology, transportation, donor, and recipient together. The operating room had to be booked. The doctors needed to be advised of the times set. An anesthetist had to be scheduled. A plane had to be chartered. The operating room at the donor hospital had to be reserved to allow for retrieval. Clearance for takeoff and landing had to be arranged. Can you begin to see the enormity of the task?

In this case one more hitch had to be overcome. God bless donors who plan to give, and we've thanked God many times for the one who shared life with Roxanne. The donor had other organs on the list for donation. The body is delicate and precise. We were told that a liver or a heart can be kept a maximum of about fourteen hours from retrieval to transplant. A kidney will last longer, but a heart-lung combination has only a brief period of time. In the latter situation, it is best for the donor and the recipient to be in the same hospital.

The heart and lungs from this body were requested for transplantation in Salt Lake City. This meant that the donor must be transported there. No problem: just a series of calls and the plane from Ontario was rerouted. The reservations of rooms and personnel were changed from one place to another, and our team was on the way—on wings of hope. Denver or Salt Lake, the city was immaterial to us. With this new development, perhaps another person would receive life. It was an uplifting thought in a stressful time. Our heartfelt appreciation goes to the family of the donor.

Precision and timing were also important. The recipient would be prepped for the transplant while the team was in the air returning with the donated liver. But the final go-ahead is never given until the retrieving doctor has analyzed the organ and given the green light. In Roxanne's case, the transplanting itself would take at least seven hours, so the coordination of the operation with the arrival of the replacement organ was crucial. When the team was still hours out of London the actual surgery would begin. Constant radio communication as to progress was essential.

With so much detail it is easy to see that the possibility of a dry run does occur. A recipient may be prepped for a transplant only to be told that the organ was found unsuitable. The frustration of such an experience holds its own anxieties. Some patients we talked to had been through several dry runs before they were given a transplanted organ.

The patient's family, however, does not simultaneously know that the process is in motion. Much of it is learned later by asking a lot of questions. We congratulate the medical and support staff for developing an efficient and successful system.

We were devastated by the severity of Roxanne's illness and the need for urgency. We were restless because we were not seeing a response to our prayers. With heavy hearts we left the hospital that night to rest, waiting for God's answer. How much longer would God keep us waiting?

6

On Sunday morning we planned to be at the hospital earlier than usual. Perhaps we could contact our church in Calgary. A call at noon would be in time for the church service back home. Our congregation was a powerful prayer force behind us, and our communication with them would be important. But what do you tell your church family when there is no positive sign, no improvement, and, humanly speaking, little hope? With heaviness we walked toward the ICU.

But wait! There was Dr. Ghent, by now not only a familiar face, but a welcome one, a person in whom we had learned to put a great deal of trust. Not only was he there, but he wanted to talk to us.

"I've got good news for you," he said. "The team is on its way to Salt Lake City to pick up a liver."

Can you imagine the relief? There was hope. It wouldn't come too late. But Dr. Ghent had more to say.

"I've also got bad news for you. We were not able

to find a compatible liver; she is a B blood type and the liver which we found is an A type. There is no time to wait. We have opted to transplant her with this liver in order to buy time. If necessary, we will transplant her again later, if or when her body rejects the first organ."

Talk about ambivalence! We wanted to cry tears of joy because the Lord had answered our prayer. But the prospect of hurt in seeing the chance of rejection, or of having to endure a second transplant, overloaded our emotions. How much could that frail little body take? If God had answered the prayers of so many people on her behalf for a liver, why could he not go one step further and answer with a compatible organ? In my wisdom, I certainly would not use such a circuitous route.

For the moment, however, there was hope, and we clung to that hope desperately. There was hope! There was progress! With Roxanne's life ebbing away, this was crucial and we believed God was making things happen. We longed to share this good news with Roxanne, but she remained unresponsive to everything.

As mentioned before, key people had a way of being there at the right time. Vickie proved this again. She knew immediately that the team was on its way and came over to share the joy with us. An embrace, tears of joy, and a few comforting words from her went a long way to ease the hurt within.

It was Sunday morning and the news had come just in time for our call to our home church prior to the morning service. Now we did have something to tell, and the whole church would be there to share the experience with us. Pastor Henry was on the phone and we spilled the news rapidly, rejoicing over this newfound answer to prayer, but also noting the concern about incompatibility.

From reports back home the emotion of the church service was an unforgettable experience for many. For a week they had prayed individually and collectively for Roxanne's health and for a replacement organ for transplantation. It isn't quite like scanning a parts list at an automobile supply center and putting a part on order! Someone dying has decided to donate an organ to another person in the hope of providing life. It is a deep concept, and we found it to be a humbling experience to be on the receiving end.

Now the answer appeared. It was too much! Was it mere coincidence that the news came on Sunday morning and could be shared with the people in the home church? I believe it wasn't just chance. It was a time of emotionally and spiritually binding our congregation together in common purpose.

There were few dry eyes in the sanctuary as Pastor Brad told the congregation how God was answering prayer. God had provided an organ. But that was only the first step. The transplant still had to be performed and the organ was in fact second best for Roxanne. More prayer was needed. A special prayer meeting was called that afternoon at the church to correspond with the timing of the operation. Both Roxanne and the medical staff would be carried on wings of prayer. God responds to that type of intercession.

At that very moment, John and Margaret came to spend time with us. That meant a two-hour drive from St. Catharines to London, but time and distance meant little to them. Unselfishly, they were there to share with us the joys and sorrows of the day. They accompanied us into the quiet room near the waiting lounge. There we praised the Lord together for his answers to prayer. Tears of joy flowed freely.

They proposed going out for dinner, and that sounded quite good. Hospital food over a long period of time has a tendency to lose some of its intrigue. We waited together until the nurses took Roxanne to the operating room at 6:15 that evening. She was a sorry sight, huge with water retention, yellow with hepatitis, tied down with tubes of various descriptions, and totally oblivious to our presence. The direction she was going, however, was all that mattered. Beyond those doors was the hope of new life.

Whoever thought of the word *patient* (or *patience*) found a most appropriate and descriptive word. It was something we would have to experience again and again. That the person in the hospital should be called a patient is almost unbelievable. They literally wait to be seen, wait to receive treatment, wait to get better, and wait to be released. How can the patient overcome the many tedious hours of waiting, longing for visitors, yearning for results, or waiting for improvements? They need patience!

The family lingers in the waiting room for endless hours. Over the course of our stay in London, the hours that were logged in waiting were absolutely staggering. But how else can one learn patience? How else can we be available to the patient if we are not nearby?

In the waiting room much sorrow and many tears are displayed by the family. So many times, and at the most inconvenient hours, we saw the emotional stress of loved ones as they waited the outcome of surgery. Or perhaps heard the sad news of a loved one having lost the battle for life. What a vivid reminder of the transient quality of life and the need for preparation for death. Our stays in the waiting rooms were an education in themselves.

Being together as a couple was of vital importance to us. The heaviness that we experienced needed to be shared and expressed. Many of our nights were late nights. We stayed with Roxanne until visiting hours were over. Ron and Eleanor were so gracious to us after we got home, and often we enjoyed each other's company until near midnight.

After they retired for the night, it was still important to call home, or simply to spend time reading Scripture and praying together. Yes, there were tears as well, but it was acceptable to cry. The emotion had to be released.

The intensity of our lives had reached its limit. We needed someone to lean on. God would not let us down. Nor would friends and acquaintances who collectively got on their knees and pleaded for healing. It was a comfort to know that God answers prayer. It helped to lessen the strain.

When we returned from dinner, Roxanne was in the operating room. Nettie and I went it to the hospitality suite which had been made available to us. It was a comfortable room with sofas and chairs, a phone, some reading material, and some coffee. We were tired and fell asleep shortly.

But stress does not allow for a long sleep; by 11:00 p.m. we were both wide awake. I paced the floor, I read the Bible, I kept running through my mind various Bible verses which promised healing or better times when the storms were over. Then we began to watch the clock. Why had they not come to tell us that the new liver had *pinked up* nicely? That is the term used by the doctors when the blood begins to flow through the new organ, bringing it back to *life*. Why were they taking so long? Were there other complications?

The next three hours seemed long then, in comparison to what they now appear in retrospect. Finally at 2:35 a.m., Dr. Wall came in, looking relatively relaxed, and gave us a summary of proceedings.

"Things went well. Roxanne made it through the operation quite well and is resting comfortably. There were no major problems and the new liver looked good when it began to function. You can go see her after the nursing staff has her cleaned up, in about half an hour."

"What about her liver? What were you able to find out? What about the donor organ? Was it good? Was it really incompatible?" We were grasping at straws. We did not want to go through this again.

"Her liver was only a ghost of its former self, perhaps performing at only 5 percent capacity."

I did not know what that meant. Was it disfigured,

deformed, and discolored, or was it simply a non-functioning organ? For the moment, it didn't matter.

Dr. Wall continued. "The donor organ was a little large so we had to make room for it."

Again my thoughts raced ahead. As a self-styled carpenter who had sawed a lot of lumber, I could only compare this with how a board is made to fit by sanding, shaving, sawing, or even forcing it into place. Nettie would likewise use stretch-and-sew techniques in her sewing room. Such surely could not be the case with a delicate organ! The body needs all of the liver, but it also needs elbowroom.

"To make room for the new liver, I took out the spleen. She won't need it in the future anyway. Go up and see her, and then go home for a rest."

He was such a thoughtful man. Alongside his professional ability and style, he had a way of making us feel at ease, even in the most trying circumstances.

We felt we were on the downhill portion of a roller coaster, gathering speed fast. A week ago we had been in Calgary. Now we had seen so much of the suffering and heartache of transplant life, along with the knowledge of technology and medicine, that it made our heads spin. But we had been given a new hope. The doctors were optimistic because of Roxanne's stability, strength, and youth. These would serve her in good stead.

The new ray of hope brightened when we went to see her at 3:00 a.m. Although she was hardly recognizable from her size, color, and the mass of tubes, she was beautiful, alive, and breathing. The new liver was working. We both felt that her color had taken on a lighter hue since we had seen her leave, some eight hours earlier. Perhaps we were imagining things.

But would she wake up? That was the next question. After all, coming out of a coma after six days does not happen easily. Even Dr. Wall had expressed concern. At this point Roxanne was listed as being in critical but stable condition.

The answer was not long in coming. When we arrived at her bedside the next morning, there were signs of movement, but her eyes were not open—yet. "Patience is a virtue," we reminded ourselves. But how long can one wait under such circumstances? Signs of movement didn't seem enough for us. We wanted more response.

John and Betty had driven down from St. Catharines that morning to spend the day with us. Like so many times before and after, friends saw the need for us to get away from the hospital for a break. They offered to take us out for lunch. It was a welcome respite, and Roxanne wouldn't miss us, for she was still not awake. But when we returned to the ICU, she had regained consciousness, and the recognition we received was overwhelming.

When Nettie approached the bed and touched her hand, Roxanne opened her eyes and turned her head. Her eyes filled with tears as she recognized her mother. What a joy! No, she did not understand what was going on, nor did she understand fully the state of her condition. But for the moment, she was awake and comprehending. That was cause for rejoicing!

Conversing with us was out of the question. The respirator tube prevented speaking, mouthing words, or even as much as swallowing a sip of water. Her means of communication for the next few days was the notepad, which she used frequently and with ingenuity. Her liver had indeed been transplanted, but her sense of humor was still her own, and it was definitely intact. As I bent over her to say something, she reached up and pinched my cheek! It was overwhelming.

She had been in a coma for six days, but her level of comprehension had been low for weeks. In one of our charaded conversations with her, she asked what had happened to her stomach. It was bandaged, and despite the drugs she sensed the pain. She still had not grasped the fact that the doctors had transplanted an organ into her body. We had repeatedly told her of her need for a transplant, even while she was still in Calgary; then again, when we arrived in London. Now as we bent over her after the fact, we told her once more. When it finally did register, she began to struggle with the full significance of such a reality.

"Do you mean someone had to die to give me their liver?" she asked. It was too much for her to accept emotionally, and the tears flowed freely. How could we support her? We had hardly had time to think of a transplant, let alone sort out the ethical ramifications in our minds. Was it only a matter of saving a life, or was it a matter of saving one life at the expense of another? Were there ethical problems involved? What, if anything, did the Bible have to say about it? With the rapid flow of events, we had not had the time to address the issue. But for the moment the important thing was to be at her side and support her as she began to struggle with the implications of transplantation.

Because of our inexperience, it seemed to us that the attitude toward organ donation by the medical staff, and by the families of needy patients, had nearly reached ghoulish proportions. It was a grim reality to us. Going into the weekend prior to Roxanne's transplant, people looked outside at the blustery and snowy weather. To them this meant a greater probability that a donor would become available—not because of false hopes or ghoulish ideas; it was a matter-of-fact approach to the problem of donations. More accidents do happen on weekends, and slippery roads also contribute to more deaths. Such talk made us uneasy until someone on the medical staff explained it to us in this way.

"No one has to die to give up a liver for you, Roxanne," they said. "Think of it rather as that donor, in his last hours before an inevitable death, giving up an organ to save the life of another. Death will occur shortly at any rate. The decision of a parent or of the patient during their lifetime is the life-giving hope which you are able to cash in on."

This explanation made it easier for us and for Roxanne to accept what had happened. Now it wasn't her life in a balance with another, depending on a doctor's decision as to whose life should be prolonged. How do you pray for an organ or a donor to appear? To pray that one becomes available is to pray for a mishap to occur. Or is it that way? Not according to the doctor's explanation. Instead, does not God in his wisdom let such a mishap occur, and through human wisdom and medical procedures make such an organ available? Regardless of which it was, Roxanne's life had been saved, and to us it was simply beautiful.

Does the Bible say anything about transplants? Can we argue in favor of or against such medical technology from the Bible? As the months rolled by, this became a topic of discussion for many in circles close to us.

What does the Bible say about the issue? Ezekiel 11:19 says, "I will take the stony heart out of their flesh and give them a heart of flesh." Ezekiel was not speaking, tongue in cheek, about transplantation. This cannot be construed as a precedent for heart transplants. A hard heart is a common picture in Scripture and depicts insensitivity to God's Word or leading. It would be bad interpretation to use that verse to justify transplanting organs.

I was unaware that the liver was even mentioned in the Bible, much less had any importance attached to it. In my devotional readings through the Old Testament, I found, however, repeated reference to the liver as a part of the acceptable portion of the sacrifice. It is strange how new ideas suddenly jump out at one as a result of experiences. Such references have always been there, but I had never been aware of them. (See Leviticus 7:4; 8:16, 25.)

There is little emphasis on healing by doctors in the Old Testament because the Lord was seen as the

Great Physician. Personal cleanliness and ritual with complete dependence on God was to heal or keep them well. Health was also tied to godly living. Exodus 15:26 reads as follows: "If you will diligently hearken to the voice of the Lord your God, and do that which is right in his eyes, and give heed to his commandments and keep all his statutes, I will put none of the diseases upon you which I put upon the Egyptians; for I am the Lord, your healer."

The guidelines set by God were complex, but clear. If his people would follow them, he would respond by being their physician with preventive medicine. The Old Testament witnesses to God's mighty deeds or miracles, many of which were health-related. None of the diseases which he allowed the Egyptians to suffer would be imposed on the Israelites. He would simply be their physician. No doubt this would be in partial reference to the plagues which both Jews and Egyptians had just witnessed (Exodus 7–12).

Even the word *doctor* or *physician* is rare in the Old Testament. Although they are present, the emphasis is on healing by God. This theme is carried into the New Testament, but there is more evidence of medicine there. Luke, we know, was a doctor (Colossians 4:14). The references to physicians in Jeremiah 8:22 and Matthew 9:12 seem to indicate that there was a general awareness of medicine being practiced, however limited it may have been (Mark 5:26). God was seen as the Great Physician.

In Jesus' ministry, the majority of his mighty works or miracles revolved around healing (Matthew

4:23-24; 8:16-17). Jesus had a desire to heal. Sometimes the record says he was moved with compassion to act on behalf of someone. Jesus often used the circumstance as an occasion for teaching.

When a leper came for healing, he believed that if Jesus wanted to, he could heal him. Jesus' response was: "I will; be clean" (Matthew 8:3).

In another example Jesus' response was slow, and as a result Lazarus died before Jesus arrived. Jesus responded by saying: "Lazarus is dead; and for your sake I am glad that I was not there, so that you may believe" (John 11:14-15).

Numerous times Jesus is seen using a healing as an object lesson in his teaching ministry. Jesus also encouraged people to come for healing, by responding to their needs when they came. How could one, after a long day, still so readily spend time with the personal needs of individuals as Jesus did? It was a sign that healing and physical comfort were important. Through God's Spirit and power, Jesus was not only able to heal their illnesses; he enjoyed doing it, and did it willingly.

Jesus had a specific ministry in healing. Later this ministry was passed on to his followers (Matthew 10:7-8). In the name of Christ, Peter and John brought healing to the lame man (Acts 3:1-10), and Paul did likewise (Acts 20:9-12; 28:8-9). But when Paul asked the Lord to remove his own "thorn . . . in the flesh," the Lord offered him grace to endure it (2 Corinthians 12:7-10).

Today Christians also claim the Lord's power to heal through prayer or the laying on of hands, or in a healing service (James 5:13-18). The Spirit endows certain persons with gifts of faith and working of miracles, so the help that comes is God's work (1 Corinthians 12:7-11). Believers may gather and offer fervent petition to God to bring deliverance when recovery is his will (James 4:15). Faith is the tool that helps us lay claim to that power; faith is openness before God and a confession that we rely upon him.

We readily accept the care of doctors, do we not? Just a peek into the medicine cabinet would indicate our dependence on pills prescribed by a doctor. And when the doctor gives advice, it sounds so logical and we are quick to apply it. We even accept the removal of some organs as a treatment, as in the case of a tonsillectomy, appendectomy, or hysterectomy. So it seems quite acceptable to live without certain organs.

But the next step may be larger than we think. Can we replace one organ with someone else's organ? Is it a different organ or is it sinful conduct that desecrates the body? What is included in keeping the temple of the Holy Spirit undefiled? I recall that when heart transplants first began, this was a crucial question. And what about the fact that someone must die in order to donate? Can this be God's will?

During our stay at University Hospital, the majority of people were supportive of the idea of transplanting. However, a few had hang-ups based on the concept of the body being the temple of God. Back we went to Scripture: "Do you not know that your body is a temple of the Holy Spirit within you, which you have from God? You are not your own; you were bought with a price. So glorify God in your body" (1 Corinthians 6:19-20).

How is this temple defiled? Is it possible to physically do something to the temple to make it less habitable by the Holy Spirit? It is simply a vessel that becomes the dwelling place of God? He indwelt those who were lame, or had a withered hand, or were blind—those who had something physically wrong with the structure of the temple. Jesus in his association with such people did not consider them any less complete than others, much less a second-class temple for the Holy Spirit.

Jesus referred to things within the body that defile. One may be corrupted by that which enters the heart—one's inner feelings and character. Evil attitudes, thoughts, motives, and impure ideas come from within to defile this body-temple. The food, which enters the mouth and passes through, does not morally defile the body (Mark 7:18-23). Thus there are clues that the temple itself can have *adjustments* made to it, but the importance is the interior of that temple, the emotional, spiritual, and moral character of a person.

As far as the acceptance of donated organs is concerned, we have no problem accepting other things supplied by a living person. A blood transfusion may be an example. A kidney shared by a close relative may be quite acceptable. Many would readily give up one kidney in order to help someone in medical difficulty. The donation of one organ for a family member seems not only natural but also honorable when the donor retains a matching organ. It is a donation without the need for the death of the giver. The body can function with one and the risk of losing the other is something that is remote from one's thoughts. After all, the body only has one heart, one liver, one pancreas. . . . The risk, therefore, is no greater with one kidney than it is with one heart.

The problem arises when a single organ, such as a liver, is desperately needed and can be given only in the case of death by the donor. In praying for an organ, am I indeed praying for the death of the donor? And is it possible that the medical diagnosis might result in one patient needing the organ more than the other, thus resulting in a transplanting, or a withholding, as the case may be? In both cases I would say no!

Medical expertise in transplantation is so well developed that we can alleviate the fear of having taken an organ before the donor is brain-dead. To ensure that this does not happen, an independent doctor declares the patient brain-dead, then the potential transplant hospitals are notified. Never is the retrieving doctor allowed to declare a potential donor as ready for donation.

Thus, nature has run its course. An accident has happened, and medicine can no longer reverse the condition of the patient. Several decisions are then made. First, is all hope of recovery gone? If so, are the organs usable in the various transplant centers? Third, do we have the family's permission to donate the organs? If the answers to these questions are affirmative, then a doctor can be sent for retrieval. The family, however, is guaranteed that all this happens in dignity and respect.

Yes, the donor must die, but not because an organ is needed. Death comes as a matter of course. It is inevitable for everyone. You and I will submit to death one day as well. However, in the moment of death, a gift is given, a chance for an extended life for someone in need of an organ. When one life ends, another begins anew. That is the value of organ donation as a way of helping in the grieving process. It has helped families deal with death.

From our perspective, that shared organ is a ray of hope for a dark and gloomy future, an extension of life for someone; for Roxanne, who could go on no further with her own, diseased organ. The donor had no further need for that liver. It was an answer to prayer.

So, how does one pray for an organ? Is it as harsh as it sounds? For us, it was a matter of praying for its availability. Roxanne needed a liver transplant at once. Yet, we had to pray for God's timing. If God was going to heal her, he would look after every aspect of that process, including the organ. In God's time, the organ would become available. He had already chosen a long way around in answering our prayer.

We prayed that God would provide an organ, in his time. We prayed that the donor would have time to deal with his or her life-and-death issues. For the donated liver, we thanked God and the family or person that was willing to give it. We praised God for the ability of the doctors to keep that slim thread of life active while we waited. We were thankful for the technology that would bring the whole process to completion. We were profoundly grateful for God's strange but marvelous ways, and we thanked him for the answer to prayer. Were we praying for someone's death to occur? I think not!

7

How does God answer prayer? I thought I had a thorough and far-reaching theology of prayer, but the proof is in the testing. On paper, or in my heart, the proof was one thing; in reality, it was another. Our belief in the power of God through answered prayer was indeed undergoing a test of fire. If it could withstand the heat, it no doubt could also become more refined.

Childhood teaching had always pointed out to me that God was the Great Physician and could heal whatever bedridden and diseased people would come to him and ask for healing in faith. This was not an aggressive form of faith healing, but rather one of quiet request, and silent waiting for the answer.

Had Jesus not healed in his ministry here on earth —people who were blind, lame, deaf, or had leprosy? And were not the dead raised (Luke 7:22)? Was not this the same Jesus Christ who "is the same yesterday and today and forever" (Hebrews 13:8)? Was not this the same Lord who had also answered similar prayers for me in the past, only on lesser matters than what was now at stake? What would he do if he were confronted with the big request?

When Roxanne first became ill, our prayers for her health were no doubt shallow and perhaps superficial. After all, teenagers often get sick and with time become well again. Few suddenly became severely ill, much less to the point of spending lengthy periods of time in the hospital. All that was needed was for nature to run its course, for the body to allow the immune system to kick in and rectify the problem that existed. How much prayer do we need to ensure such a natural procedure?

What was at stake here, for me, was the same attitude that is beginning to pervade our society regarding our need to pray for our daily bread. Do we still need to pray for daily bread if we have a secure job? Does our daily bread come from God or does it come from our secure payrolls? Do we need to pray for health if the body has the built-in system to correct itself, and with technology forging ahead in the area of transplants?

There were other things in our favor. The medical staff was excellent, and the medical technology had never been this good. Coupling these things together with God's ability to answer the prayer of an honest person on his knees, surely my daughter had an excellent chance at survival. We have a lot of built-in backup systems.

As her health deteriorated, our individual and corporate prayers increased in fervency. Yes, God could hear; he could heal, but at the moment he had chosen not to, or at least to delay the answer. But God was still one who answered prayer, so we refused to let up in our requests. Had Paul not said in one of his letters to the church, "Pray without ceasing" (1 Thessalonians 5:17, KJV)? Had Jesus not said, "Ask, and you will receive, that your joy may be full" (John 16:24)?

But the intensity of the prayers brought no change in the prognosis of her condition. It became necessary for my own sake that I review in my mind the promises made in Scripture about the Lord's ability, and his willingness to answer prayer. I gave this to myself for a *homework assignment.*

Tied to the concept of answered prayer is the mystery, Why is God allowing me to suffer so? While we were still in Calgary that question was raised in our bedside conversation. What could God have in mind by allowing Roxanne to experience the pain and discomfort of being bedridden? What about the friends who enjoyed full health and happiness, without the hardships she felt? "What is so fair about the way God is treating me?" was her question.

Our discussion brought us around to the topic of bitterness. Understandably, Roxanne was bitter at this "unfairness." In the most simple and direct way I knew, I pointed out to her that extended bitterness against God was not good, regardless of the feelings she might have that stemmed from her illness (Hebrews 12:15).

God does not owe us health, happiness, wealth, or

fame. He is the supreme Sovereign, and he has the right to choose, or be gracious to, or show mercy to whom he will (Exodus 33:19). And to allow whatever he feels appropriate for the person and the situation (2 Corinthians 12:7-10). We need to trust God even when it seems like he is slaying us (Job 13:15, KJV) or abandoning us (Psalm 22).

One night during the first week of her hospital stay in Calgary, before we left for home we prayed together as we would do so many times in the next months. When Roxanne prayed, it was a genuine request for forgiveness of her attitude of bitterness regarding God's unfairness to her as a teenager in allowing her to suffer more than others. It was only a short time later that she requested that the elders of the church be called to lay on hands and pray for her in accordance with James 5. This was planned for Saturday afternoon.

My own heart needed preparation for such an event. I would be present in a double role, as father and as an elder. It was a new experience for me, and I felt that God needed to show me a few things first. I spent that Saturday morning in spiritual preparation, first in fasting, then in Scripture reading and prayer. God was at work in my life.

My thoughts were guided to the Gospel of John, where it almost seems directed toward a slow learner. Four times in the space of several chapters Jesus says the same thing: "If you ask anything in my name, I will do it" (John 14:13-14; 15:7, 16; 16:23-26). Other passages were added to the list, including, "The effectual fervent prayer of a righteous man has great power in its effects" (James 5:16, KJV/RSV).

Several things were becoming real to me. First, I was being encouraged to ask. Maybe I was the slow learner, and needed to be told repeatedly that a genuine request was in order. This would be a test as to whether I could keep it simple, genuine, and sincere.

Also, I realized that I had to take God's will into account and ask accordingly. What if this did not include Roxanne's healing? If it was a battle of the wills, I certainly knew where I stood. I had always given verbal assent to doing God's will, but when it came to the crunch, what would I rather have? My choice was not to have a sick child. How much less could I face the prospect of death? But I was at the argumentative stage, debating with God at every turn. I still saw things from a human standpoint and not from God's.

Corporate prayer seemed so powerful that I believed God could not allow Roxanne to remain ill. Hundreds of people were praying for us as a family. But I knew that people, even children and teenagers, were bedridden for long periods of time, and some did in fact succumb to death. Why did God allow this to happen? Would he allow this in Roxanne's case?

The timing was something that I tried to give totally to God as well. He might answer today, or maybe tomorrow, or even years from now. And the reply might not be in the same form that I expected it to be. So many times in the next months I would repeat the words to the song: "In his time. . . . He makes all things beautiful in his time." There may be only partial healing, and that may be next year. What if God chose to answer in this way?

Finally, it became apparent to me that, if the answer to our prayers was not complete recovery, God would be there to uphold us with his everlasting arms, to carry us if necessary. "Underneath are the everlasting arms" (Deuteronomy 33:27). He would not allow me to be swamped by the sheer frustration or grief of the burden (Isaiah 43:1-2).

Psalm 32:6-7 says it so well: "Therefore let every one who is godly offer prayer to thee; at a time of distress, in the rush of great waters, they shall not reach him. Thou art a hiding place for me, thou preservest me from trouble; thou dost encompass me with deliverance." These Scriptures were seeds that would sprout and give rise to the hope on which we as a couple would live over the next months.

Thus with renewed hope I went to the hospital early to help Roxanne prepare for the prayer time with the elders. Nettie was working that Saturday, so I was initiated into something new, that I would later learn how to do better. I had to wash Roxanne's hair. At this point her strength was hardly enough to stagger to the washroom around the corner, or to lean on the sink long enough to have me wash her tangled mat of hair. It was done ever so gingerly. Then she leaned back in bed, where she anxiously waited for the elders to come.

I shared with her the joy of promise in God's answers to prayer which he had given and for the healing he would give. The elders came, and we prayed together. It was a fervent prayer, and we believed God would answer. We held him to his promise.

It was an uplifting experience for all of us, especially for Roxanne. But there were no immediate results. Her color did not lose its yellow tinge and take on a more healthy pink. Her fever did not quickly subside, nor did her strength return in a spurt of energy. The doctors did not change their diagnosis; it still was "severe liver failure," with hope for a turnaround being more and more dependent on a miracle.

I continued to struggle with God's timing. There was no doubt in my mind that God would heal; he was capable of that. But patience was a necessity and I still had not attained a high level in this area. When word came of the need for a transplant, I prayed more earnestly for healing, but it seemed that God would continue at his own pace.

If the choice were up to me, there would be no need to travel to London, no need for a transplant, and no need for all the suffering. Just a short stay in the hospital and then back home. But God had other plans. Character and patience are built on hardships. God would have us wait, and wait, and wait.

With the final decision to go to London and the preparations came the grim reality that God had chosen not to answer now. We responded by calling the elders again. By this time Roxanne was no longer comprehending her surroundings. They formed a complete circle around the bed, and the prayer was direct. "God we expect an answer. We know you have the ability. We want your will to be done." Still

God withheld the answer, and off we went to London.

As Roxanne's condition deteriorated, I began to argue with God. "You promised, Lord." In my mind and in our Scripture reading we reviewed again the verses that told of promises of answered prayer. But it wasn't until Nettie and I had reached our lowest point emotionally that we were able to say, "Lord, if you don't want to heal her, then go ahead, take her, and thank you for the years you have given her to spend with us." We could now pray more freely for the Lord's will to be done.

It was a difficult step to take, but that is what the Lord expects of his followers; they dare not hold anything back. He wants complete control of our lives. It was a turning point in our prayer life. Now we were able to pray more readily for the Lord's will to be done, regardless of the consequences. No, we did not give up praying for her recovery, but we had a calm assurance that the Lord's will was being fulfilled.

As others prayed, they often shared their concerns and experiences with us. Someone mentioned to us that in her concern for Roxanne, she had asked the Lord to wake her every time Roxanne needed prayer throughout the night. She had prayed numerous times during her waking hours. History reports events where individuals felt the need to pray at a specific time, only to find out later that a specific need existed. We adapted a similar approach: "God, if she needs us, please make us available for prayer."

One morning after a restless night, Nettie and I

compared notes. She had fallen asleep immediately from the exhaustion of the day. For me it was a long night of watching the clock and spending time in prayer. I remember checking the clock shortly before 3:00 a.m. Then I fell asleep. Nettie woke up at 3:00 a.m. and spent the hours till morning waking and praying. What a way to guarantee a round-the-clock prayer vigil! I couldn't have planned it better myself. We may never know how critical that night of prayer was in her healing process.

Corporate prayer was an extremely important aspect. Scripture points to the power of praying concertedly (Matthew 18:19-20; Acts 4:23-31). Back home in Calgary prayer chains in numerous churches went into action as soon as new requests were voiced. Before long we became aware of chains of believers who joined in prayer for Roxanne's health from as far away as Singapore. By now our prayer support doubtlessly numbered in the thousands.

Friends and acquaintances were passing on the information they knew, and new prayer cells went into action on Roxanne's behalf. It was both humbling and encouraging to find that people were praying for our family. We were sure that such a great source of power could not go unnoticed by God. We made a point of keeping prayer chains as up-to-date as possible so others could pray intelligently.

Reversals in Roxanne's health often were times of testing for us. Our first reactions were always to check to see if our prayer life had slipped in fervency and frequency. Back we would go to God's promises, back to the prayer chains, and back to our knees to intercede further. Each time we would see a gradual improvement, at which time our pleading would turn to praise. Once again, it was a sign to us that the answer to prayer that God was providing was also a hint of God's timing. In *his* time, he would heal.

Many answers to small prayers happened during this experience. They were more easy to understand. They seemed so simple for God to handle, so why did he not prove himself powerful in the big answers? Three such experiences revolved around the need for financing, a problem which understandably was a concern.

In my first trip back to London, I felt that I was needed there, but did not have sufficient funds for airfare. In my prayers, I asked God to give me the assurance that I was to go. I told God I would travel if there was enough money available to pay for a ticket, to be purchased on short notice. When I checked the price of the ticket and our finances, there was still $2.02 left over. In faith, I went ahead, and before I left, there was more funding.

The second experience also revolved around a plane ticket. After Roxanne's stay in London dragged on into its seventh month, I began to plan another trip. My requested sign from the Lord this time was that I must be able to purchase a fare for roughly half the price paid on the short-notice tickets. Although several airlines said it was impossible, one such ticket became available. Coincidence, you say? I believe not. I think God hears and answers such prayer. These small incidents were a challenge to me regarding the larger ones.

A third experience revolved around the paying of a substantial bill worth several hundred dollars. People had been very generous in sharing with us, but as you can imagine, costs escalated quickly. We discussed the situation over the phone. Nettie and I decided to go ahead and pay the bill despite the fact that it would drain our account.

Our finances were often a part of our prayers, and God was gracious to us. Friends, colleagues, and acquaintances often rallied to the cause financially. They were so good to us! As I sent off the check I prayed again that God would provide the necessary funds. The next day, an identical amount arrived in the mail from a friend. Coincidental? Again, I believe not.

My faith in God was being strengthened, in the small, everyday experiences. From these, I was learning that trusting God in the small things can then also lead to trust in the big things. "Oh, for a faith that will not shrink!"

8

Post-transplant time is ruled by routines. Everything must be precise, accurate, and on time. The hustle and bustle of the intensive-care unit (ICU) was enough to make our heads spin, even with only the short periods of time we were allowed in. Luckily for us, rules are made to be broken; our visits were much longer than prescribed.

The staff had a strong feeling that the presence and communication of family members were crucial to recovery. It is important for us to talk to sick persons, stroke their hands, be there, attempt to help them understand the pain and discomfort they are going through, and assure them of our love. On that pretext we were given extra time to spend with Roxanne. Nurses were busy with prescribed duties, but we found that few of them felt that as parents we were a hindrance to their progress with the patient. It was rewarding to both parents and patient. We made good use of the time and attempted not to overstay our welcome.

Getting accustomed to an ICU was a harrowing experience. Though Steve had taken us through the motions prior to the transplant, it was more realistic and harrowing when our own child was a part of the maze of tubes, bags, bottles, beeps, groans, and hisses. Standing in the entrance to the unit reminded me of my days on the farm when on a clear summer night the air was alive with the songs of frogs from a nearby pond. The only thing missing was the carefree attitude that went with those childhood days. Here the reality was far from carefree; it dealt with life and death.

A part of getting used to the procedures of intensive care is the protocol. Only members of the family were to come and see the patient, except when one member would escort a friend in. Only two visitors were allowed at one time, and the time limit was to be five minutes per hour. Hospital gowns had to be worn backwards. These were not the most pleasant in color and style but seemed effective in guarding against spread of outside germs. Hands had to endure a previsit and a postvisit scrub, to avoid further contamination. We were told that earlier rules had been even more strict on masks and isolation procedures. Now, however, as transplant technology had improved, these were no longer deemed necessary.

One of the most stressful places in the hospital is the intensive-care waiting room. This was particularly true at University Hospital because this room services the ICU, the operating room, and the recovery room. Stress was quite apparent on an average day as we waited with others for news or progress reports. It isn't hard to make friends under such conditions, particularly if the same people show up day after day. Many binding friendships were begun in that waiting room, many heartaches shared, tears shed, and new hopes expressed. To remain positive, one must verbalize hope. Our hope was deep-rooted; it was anchored in God, who had the power to heal. We shared that hope with others.

In the waiting room we met Roberto, who had accompanied his wife to London for an operation to repair an aneurysm. They had come from Uruguay, drained their bank account, and knew not a word of English. He needed friendship desperately. My newly purchased little English-Spanish dictionary served us well as we charaded our way through numerous conversations. It was one of many meaningful friendships which developed there. Perhaps not much was said, but much was experienced.

What a way to turn eighteen! Roxanne's birthday was on January 28. But she was in no mood to eat cake or blow out candles. Nor could her respirator blow out her candles for her. The mood was not the most conducive to celebration, and yet it should have been. She was on the road to recovery, and that was reason for thanksgiving.

Despite the fact that birthday trappings are important, they simply were not possible in the ICU. But the staff was aware of the occasion and responded in a lovely manner. Steve brought up some balloons for her, and numerous nurses gathered around to sing happy birthday to her. There were cards from back home, and there was a birthday cake—only a plastic blow-up model, but nevertheless a cake. Presents and celebration would have to wait until next year.

Lying in bed intubated with a respirator, and immobilized by numerous tubes, pins, and tapes, has to be frustrating. Imagine your natural, involuntary reactions to having a tube down your throat, or an arm tied to the bed to limit the movement. Now compound the problem with drowsiness from the anesthetic and from morphine, given to kill the pain. Imagine the dull throbbing ache in the abdomen that refuses to go away.

The nurses, while doing an excellent job, nonetheless remain the ogres in your eyes. They wake you at unrealistic hours, give you needles, help you with intimate moments on the bedpan, and ask you to lie still and cooperate. Others come with regularity to take your blood or to wheel you off for an X-ray. Add to this the bright lights, the hisses and beeps of the equipment as it monitors your progress. Do you begin to see the picture?

In such a condition, the patient is not accountable for her own actions. This was also true for Roxanne. On several occasions she pulled out tubes in her restless state. Reinsertion meant looking for new veins or reintubating the respirator. The staff would often wait for some time to check if she needed that form of support. On the day that she pulled out her respirator tube, she was able to breathe on her own for several hours. Then she became so exhausted that she begged for it. When they gave it back to her, she fell asleep almost immediately from exhaustion.

Her recovery was slow for a number of reasons. She had been extremely ill and her body was full of poisons from her diseased liver. She had been in a deep coma for at least five or six days. Her new liver was incompatible and the doctors were making every effort to avoid rejection.

They put her on heavy doses of ALG, an antirejection agent which paralyzes the immune system. No rejection can take place if the immune system cannot recognize false tissue. (My information is that new medication has become available in the treatment of transplant recipients.) ALG was used for several days until the gradual switch was made to cyclosporine, a milder form of immunosuppressant, as well as Imuran and prednisone.

We soon learned that rejection was the word most to be feared in transplant circles. Therefore, drastic treatment was being given.

A second method was used to attempt to stem the tide of rejection. Blood feresis is literally an exchange of the blood plasma in the patient's body. This process was done every forty-eight hours for a week, in the attempt to put the blood and the new organ more or less on the same footing. Blood was taken from an artery and pumped through a centrifuge to separate the plasma from the rest of the blood. Her plasma was then discarded and new blood pumped in. In the process the strength of her antibodies was reduced and thus the possibility of rejection was not as great.

Personal care suffers when one is bedridden for such a period of time. For Roxanne, it was nine days between shampoos. It is one thing to have dirty hair; it is quite another to have it matted and tangled due to length and lack of care. In hospital circles it has affectionately become known as "bedhead." Mom came to the rescue quickly when the nurse unsuccessfully attempted to untangle the matted mess.

A haircut under such circumstances would be similar to the youngster who must get the gum trimmed out of his hair. We felt there must be a better way, and Nettie set about to untangle it a few strands at a time. What a pleasure to see a smile on her face when her hair was washed and neatly combed.

We tried to prepare ourselves for the inevitable. The day came when we had to face rejection episodes. It happens with every transplant, and Roxanne's case was no exception. The doctors told us repeatedly that it is natural to experience rejection, but that in most cases it can be countered with more suppressants.

The term used in medical circles is that "the enzymes are up." We arrived at the hospital one day to hear that message from the nurse regarding Roxanne. I thought I was strong and would not readily succumb to such emotional stress. However, for the first time I had to hurry out of the ICU to look after my own needs. I didn't want the nurses to have the added burden of having to care for a father as well.

We struggled with this new concept, but the doctors simply took it in stride, prescribed heavier doses of drugs, and watched for positive results. To them it was routine. A check later that day proved that our fears were unfounded. It was only a minor rejection.

Disappointments are keenly felt by patients eager for progress. Between making positive statements and realistic evaluations, the doctors are often caught in a situation where they create false hopes for the patient. Roxanne was so anxious to get out of the ICU, and the medical staff agreed that it should be soon.

If it doesn't happen on schedule, the patient may develop what is called "ICU syndrome." This is a situation where the constant medical care and the noise of the unit keeps the patients awake and begins to wear on their nerves. They need sleep, but in this unit there is constant motion, light, and noise. If the optimism of a short stay in the unit is thwarted by complications, the patient finds it a hard pill to swallow.

This was the case for Roxanne. Her stay in ICU was prolonged because of complications. Several times we heard "maybe tomorrow," but the next day brought with it more concerns which kept her there. Many tears were the result of hopes dashed due to lack of progress.

While crying she would exclaim, "I'll never get out of here!" She was frustrated with the speed of her recovery, not with the care in the unit. Staff continued to give first-rate treatment. They need to be commended!

Time in the hospital for patients and their families is counted in milestone experiences. After the transplant the next event was for her to wake up, then for her to breathe without the respirator, then begin to talk on her own. Finally it was the move out of ICU and into MOTS, the step-down unit for multiple organ transplant patients. It was a relief, after twelve days in the ICU, to go to a unit where the care given is on a level between that of the ICU and the general ward. Now she could relax more, sleep more, and have more company, yet have excellent care.

Setbacks are hard to take. Rejection is a reversal which is expected in a transplant procedure. In Roxanne's case the heavy doses of drugs led to another problem. When we entered the hospital the next day, we heard an emergency call over the public-address system. By the time we reached MOTS, nurses, doctors, and technicians were converging toward the unit from everywhere. "Someone's in trouble," we thought, but all too soon we became aware that Roxanne's bed was the center of the commotion. Doctors were quick in responding to our worried glances.

"Roxanne has developed a big problem. She has gone into seizures, and we think it is because the heavy doses of drugs have lowered her tolerance level. No, we don't think these are epileptic, nor do we think that they will have a lasting effect. But we can't tell. It's simply too soon to draw conclusions. She will have to go back to intensive care."

What a way for a daughter to surprise her parents who are on their way in for a visit! We were stunned, even though we thought that little could shake us anymore. Was this a further test of our faith? Was God not finished with us yet? Back we went to the ICU, but under much more tense circumstances. The seizures had left Roxanne disoriented and frustrated, struggling with all her lines and equipment.

In her state of semiconsciousness she vacillated between wanting us to help her, and rejecting every form of help we offered. She begged for things that we couldn't decipher, or that made no sense to us. Our attempts to understand and assist brought more frustration. Test after test was performed, and each came back with positive results. What a blessing that those two days were wiped from her memory. We would love to forget them as well.

Back in the MOTS, things progressed at a slow but steady pace. She began to be more conversant, no longer counting only on the nod to speak for her. It was good to hear partial sentences again. Even her voice, which was a mere whisper as a result of a lengthy bout with the respirator, was becoming stronger. Next she took a short stint in the chair beside her bed, then a step or two with the help of the nurse and physiotherapist. Even walking had to be relearned and took great effort. But a major milestone was the ride in a wheelchair, albeit accompanied by an IV pole. Such is the measure of success and progress.

After four weeks Roxanne was able to move to a ward. She attempted to be brave now that some of the expert care and attention received in the transplant unit would be missing. On the main ward, sharing the room with another patient, she would have to fend for herself much more.

We had been in London for a month and the separation of family members was beginning to take its toll, both at home as well as in London. John and Tina were doing an excellent job parenting our kids back home. Bell Canada was the other partner in helping to keep our family together. Our thinking from the start had been that communication with members of the immediate family as well as the church family was important, regardless of the cost. However, before long we began to look for cheaper ways to make long-distance calls. Eleven in the evening at London was 9:00 p.m. in Calgary. If we waited for the cheaper rates after 11:00, it was still relatively early at home. Then we could talk to family members at a reduced rate. However, even reduced fees add up.

Teachers' convention in Calgary brought a natural break from school for Corinne and Gwen, so we began to work on the possibility of having them come to Ontario to see us. We felt it would be good for several reasons. We had been away for a month, and young teenagers need their parents, particularly in such trying circumstances. They also needed to see Roxanne's situation firsthand in order to understand it better. And Mom and Dad were getting lonely for them at this point.

Although finances were beginning to be a problem, we felt and prayed that this would be possible. Before we had time to buy the tickets, our care group back home had the same idea. We were closely attached to them and had met with them on a weekly basis for Bible study and prayer. With a little planning and a lot of help from the group, the travel plans were finalized. Our daughters would leave Calgary late Wednesday night, on the red-eye special, and then I would accompany them back home on the following Monday. The specter of work, to put bread on the table, was beginning to loom large.

We had decided to pick up the girls at Toronto rather than have them go through a transfer of planes and fly into London. We would leave London on Wednesday afternoon and take a motel in Toronto, to be there when the early-morning flight arrived.

But friends continued to insist on being so good to us. Dorothy was Pastor Gordon's wife. Her parents lived in Mississauga, which is only minutes away from the airport. She insisted that we stay at her parents' home for the night. The fact that we had never met was no problem to her or her parents. They saw us as a couple in need and responded by providing what they could, in this case a bed for the night. What a loving couple! They give us not only lodging, but also breakfast for all four of us after the girls arrived. Such love cannot be repaid. We owe many such debts of gratitude.

It was a treat to see our daughters. They were being escorted by a purser who spotted them and took them under his wing as he wheeled another passenger to the carousel to pick up his baggage. We were relieved to see that they had been well looked after on the flight. It had been an adventure for them. Nonetheless, the excitement did not last long before the exhaustion of the trip left them sound asleep. The trip back to London was conducive to such relaxation.

Some of the girls' feelings had begun to surface as they attempted to struggle through the experience of the transplant, and with it the complications of family separation. Their reactions were remote, because they had not seen any of the experience firsthand. Gwen expressed herself to her teacher in a classroom assignment in the form of a poem. It was beautiful!

Life

"I didn't think it would ever happen, especially not
 today,"
Is a very common line that we so often say.

As I bent down low and gently kissed her,
To think this frail girl could actually be my sister.
There was pain in her eyes as she tried to be brave.
Alone in her hospital bed, she looked very tired and
 grave.

Off to London she flew in a hurry
And left everything at home in a flurry.
She was in great pain because she needed a liver fast;
If she didn't get one soon, she surely wouldn't last.

Life is something we so often take for granted.
My sister got a second chance because she was trans-
 planted.
Life is very fragile, so handle with care,
Because you never know when life might not be there.

The weekend went by too quickly. Corinne and Gwen had to learn the routine of hospital life, and how Roxanne fit into it. The number of visitors in Roxanne's room now suddenly doubled. She was still a weak patient, and it was simply too much for her to deal with the constant visits. For teenagers, boredom is common and hospital life as a visitor is no exception. But the girls had brought a lot of books, homework, and crafts along to occupy the hours of waiting. It was a strain for them to be with Roxanne, because of her weak condition and because of their failure to fully understand her condition. I'm convinced they grew older and wiser in that one weekend.

As we arrived at the hospital from Toronto, the hospital beautician was giving Roxanne a haircut while she was still attached to the IV dangling from a pole. That was more activity than we had seen in a long time and the girls were there to share it with us. They hustled about talking, laughing, and sharing things with her that they had not been able to do for six weeks. But Roxanne was still too weak, and too sick, to enjoy all the commotion. The excitement was short-lived.

Monitoring vitals was still a top priority for the doctors. As a result, we did not wonder that Roxanne's blood level was low; she was compelled to give so much away for tests. That afternoon, after the results of the tests were in, there was another flurry of activity around her bed as Dr. Grant and his resident doctor came in. We knew they meant business by their stride and urgency. The explanation was quick in coming.

"Roxanne has gone into major rejection. Her enzymes are very high. She must go back to the transplant unit so we can administer more medical aid, including higher doses of antirejection drugs, and have her vitals constantly on the monitor. We will be putting her on OKT3 to attempt to reverse the rejection."

We were stunned. From previous discussions with medical staff and from reading we knew the power of OKT3. It was known as the "nuclear weapon" of transplant medicine, a drug that was used only as a last resort and was expected to reverse rejection. Those who understood the meaning of its choice dreaded its use. Things must be bad if they were going to try that drug. When it was mentioned, shock was a common facial expression. I understand that it is now used quite regularly, but we were afraid. How does one handle discouragement and emotions at a time such as this? How could we be positive to her if we knew the dangerous situation she was in?

With heavy hearts we cleaned up her room and accompanied her back to the transplant unit. She was so dejected, and we attempted to cheer her up. However, reversals like moving from the ward back to MOTS are not easy to cover up. We wiped the tears, we prayed, we read more Scripture, and then it was time to leave her alone with her fears. Visiting hours were over for the day.

More prayers were needed and we called home, where the requests were immediately placed on the prayer chains again. We prayed earnestly, as we had so many times before. I told God he dare not let us down after he had taken us so far. And God stands by his Word.

That night it was late when we retired. The nursing staff in the transplant unit had always encouraged us to phone anytime, regardless of the hour, to see if there was progress or change. When we called, we were overjoyed. Before they applied OKT3, they had done a skin test to see whether the drug was acceptable to the body. Roxanne had shown a reaction to it, so they had decided against using it. In its place they had used Solu-Medrol, another antirejection agent. That was an answer to prayer. Another answer came the next morning when we phoned again. Her temperature was down. Her enzyme level had corrected itself, and she was resting comfortably. What a relief! Was it mere coincidence?

Before the girls and I left to go back to Calgary, we had hoped and prayed for a major breakthrough, like a ride in the wheelchair for Roxanne, with a trip to the illustrious cafeteria. With such setbacks, this prospect had dimmed considerably. But the new medicine did its job well, and the dream was realized. We did make a family trek to the cafeteria. Gwen and Corinne took turns pushing the wheelchair and the IV pole, which by this time had been dubbed "Fat Jack." Mom and Dad trailed behind and held doors and elevators open. That was a much treasured family outing.

Just before we left, a new problem began to appear. Roxanne became aware of substantial swelling and pain in small sections of her abdominal incision. To her it was understandably frightening, and somehow my medical "expertise" did not assuage those fears. But doctors were there when needed, and Dr. Wall was a welcome sight, having arrived back from a week of well-deserved holidays. His examination revealed the first signs of a hematoma (a swelling containing blood). This lack of healing caused by the heavy doses of immunosuppressants hounded her for succeeding months. Such pockets of minor infection had to be reopened and drained in order to heal properly.

Then it was time to say good-bye. We had developed a bond based on love and cultured in hardship. Tears were expected. Not only were we interrupting a close togetherness, but it could be a long time before we would see each other again. The painful good-byes were made the previous night; our flights left early the next morning.

Leaving Roxanne in her condition was one thing. Leaving Nettie to face the routine of visits and the pressure of decisions by herself was another. Going home to take on the role of a single parent of two teenage girls who were hurting was still another. Again we found comfort in God's Word: When the trials come, you will not be swamped (Isaiah 43:1-2).

9

Our separate lives began the next morning with the late departure of the plane to Toronto due to a snowstorm. It turned out to be a day of delays. What under normal circumstances was a mere five hours' flying time, London to Calgary, became a twelve-hour experience. First there was the wait in London due to the bad weather. Next there was a postponement in Toronto due to mechanical problems on the plane.

The girls spent this time of frustration knitting. Finally we were rescheduled on another plane and arrived in Calgary in the early evening. What a change of pace! From the routine of hospital life, I suddenly found myself as a single parent with regular housekeeping chores. I was also back in the real world. Tomorrow, it was back to work in the grim reality of catch-up and cope in the classroom.

In hospital, meanwhile, Roxanne encountered another scare early that Monday morning. She had scarcely recovered from the side effects of drugs that caused her seizures, when she developed an imbalance in her sugar level. She had been on insulin to help maintain her metabolism. Early that morning she went into insulin reaction and had to be given sugar immediately to guard against a coma. The new medications administered as a result of the latest rejection were simply too hard on the sugar level.

Unlike the problems a week earlier, this time Roxanne was aware of the difficulty, and it left her quite shaken. It was another reminder of the delicate balance that had to be maintained on the road to recovery.

With the rest of the family gone, life became a daily routine of boring occurrences for Roxanne. Day after day, the long-awaited return to health still seemed so far away. The hours were long, the pain was severe, and the depression was so deep that coping became a full-time job for both mother and daughter. Nettie helped to keep the emotions up and dried the tears that often came. She began to look around for new ways to do this. Knitting took up part of the slack, as did watching TV, or renting a video. Sometimes it was the anticipation of talking to the family at home, or waiting for letters and cards in the daily mail. Nettie took attention off the pain and cares and thereby reduced tensions for the moment.

Healing was slow. Hematomas continued to develop along the incision. Because her immune system was so suppressed, the healing process had slowed. These pockets of infection had to be opened and drained. Before long much of the incision stood open. But the doctors continued to be positive about her progress in spite of such minor setbacks.

A recuperating patient must exercise. Physiotherapy was planned for the frail patient. The therapists had been around all along, vibrating her to help clear her lungs, helping her begin to walk, encouraging her to cough and to faithfully use her spirometer. Walking was therapeutic, particularly when it took such effort simply to motor to the washroom.

With the advent of technology, the exercise room could be brought to the bed. Before long, Roxanne was lying on her back, peddling an exercise bike attached to the end of her bed. How convenient! Arm exercises could likewise be done with the help of small weights and elastic strips. Loretta was her therapist and lacked nothing in ingenuity. Few excuses were good enough for not exercising on any given day.

As her strength increased, she was then able to do her biking in the therapy room on the sixth floor. First it was small distances on shaky legs, then longer distances, one kilometer, then two, and even more. It was reassuring to see that strength was returning. Even the wheelchair came into disuse as the distance between her room and other points of progress were traveled on foot.

Minor rejections happened occasionally, but the response of the doctors was simple: raise the cyclosporine level, first to 450, then to 525, then 625. Rejection was not the only reason for such high doses. The levels were varied, depending on the amount of absorption by the body, which was influenced by episodes of nausea or diarrhea.

Accompanying such rejections was a high fever, some pain, stomach discomforts, and extreme weakness. "Start her on Imuran," another steroid, was the response. Each time when rejection was brought under control the levels were again stabilized. We were beginning to gain confidence that there was indeed light at the end of the tunnel. Hope began to look more like a reality. God was indeed responding to our prayers. Doctors were living up to the ability which had been ascribed to them before we came.

Progress was slow but sure. The incision suddenly began to heal more rapidly, appetite and strength began to return, as did assurance that a normal life might be a possibility. Soon Roxanne was able to walk to the cafeteria on her own. Such a trip still required a rest stop, but it nevertheless was a major accomplishment. Then came the day when she was allowed her first leave of absence for a few hours. What an excitement for her! What a challenge for Nettie!

Teenagers and a craving for hamburgers seem nearly synonymous, so it was no surprise when the first planned stop was to be at McDonalds. The plan was to pick up some burgers and go to the Hunnifords for a relaxing snack. But Roxanne was due for a culture-shock. The fastest thing on wheels in the hospital was a stretcher, or perhaps a wheelchair out of control. Now she had to readjust to cars whizzing along a street at considerably exaggerated stretcher speeds. It was more than she could handle.

Another problem developed. The Hunnifords'

house had a two-step entryway. Up to this point Roxanne had been walking down the halls, but had neither the reason nor the strength to use any stairs. Suddenly she was required to negotiate several to get into the house. On her own strength it was impossible. With Nettie's help on one arm, and a firm hold with the other hand on the door, which swung out over the step, they were able to negotiate the stairs—a major accomplishment.

When the next move was discussed, she quickly responded, "Get me back to the hospital."

But the insecurity didn't last long. Roxanne and Nettie went to look for Medic Alert bracelets and even made a few short sightseeing trips, with stops for donuts. There was still a psychological barrier: standing or walking in the hospital was easier than doing the same thing on the sidewalk, in the real world. It was similar to the travel speed, which still bothered her. More readjustment would be necessary.

For a patient to recuperate is a reasonable expectation. However, when it doesn't happen at the expected rate of progress, it becomes discouraging. For the next month there was progress, but it was slow. There were times of spiked temperatures, stomach disorders, and poor appetite. But then, there was improvement.

The day arrived when Dr. Wall suggested discharge from the hospital. It was a happy day, but not without its apprehensions. A dependency on doctors and hospital had begun to develop. She was torn between wanting to leave and the fear of leaving.

Would she be able to cut the proverbial apron strings?

Her discharge came on March 31, ending a two-month stay in the hospital. It was a new lease on life. She had shopping to do, places to see. Limited strength, however, slowed down such excursions, and often escapades were interrupted by rest stops in malls or early returns to go home to bed. She was still a weak girl, and only time would help increase her strength.

Chills came easily. After her first shower, she literally shook for hours while her body temperature was restored with the help of blankets. Baths or showers had to be quick and heavy clothing had to be available. The car had to be warm, and little walking could be done outdoors. That would simply have to wait for better health, better weather, or both.

Roxanne visited the hospital daily. Every two days she needed to donate blood for tests to see if her cyclosporine levels were good. This had to be done before she took her morning dose of that medicine. Physiotherapy, to help build body muscle, stamina, and strength, was best done under the watchful and skilled eyes of the therapists at the hospital.

The liver-transplant support group met every Friday morning. They had strengthened us so much, and we wanted to encourage others going through the same ordeal. This group had introduced us to Transplant International, an organization that helps families of transplant patients. Through publications and information meetings, it promotes acceptance of organ transplantation. We were beginning to see what they stood for. Perhaps we could now be of assistance to them.

Visits to other patients and their families had become routine and could not be forfeited now. They had given of themselves and supported us when we needed them; Nettie and Roxanne reciprocated in kind. Their friendship was valuable. Life outside the hospital became a busy affair.

Frustrations continued for Roxanne as an outpatient. A lot of things can be blamed on the long stay in the hospital, but it was still a stable thing in her frail life. She still tired easily. The security of knowing that a medical opinion was only an arm's length away was suddenly taken away. A headache or a fever must now be dealt with in home-remedy style, and not in a call-the-nurse fashion. So a considerable amount of anxiety still existed.

When going home to Calgary was mentioned, we became aware of another concern. Would we be able to cut our medical ties with London and feel comfortable with the support in Calgary? We were assured that the communication lines would remain open between the two cities and Dr. Wall would continue to make the decisions based on tests performed in Calgary. In theory this sounded great; in practice it left us with some anxiety which could be taken away only through a proven track record.

Disappointments continued. Dr. Wall had already set a date for departure when Roxanne developed a high fever and several major symptoms of rejection. Instead of going home, she was readmitted to University Hospital for a few days while the medical staff continued to do its fine-tuning. The cyclosporine was now more than the maintenance level needed for her body; the excess was causing problems. A few adjustments and she was released again.

Another date was set, and finally the day arrived for her to return home. What a feeling! How can it be described? Mom would have to be responsible for the packing and the luggage, but Roxanne would need little help for the boarding and transfer of planes. Wheelchairs were available if needed, but she was out to prove a point. They were not needed.

On April 28, after more than three months in London, Roxanne and Nettie traveled home. Can you imagine their feelings? It would be so good to see the family at home! What about the church people who had prayed so hard? What about the personal friends who had not seen her during this entire time? Would everyone be as happy to see her as she was to be home? It was a tense moment as everyone waited for the happy reunion.

10

Good news travels quickly, and this was no exception. Friends and family gathered at the airport for the joyful reunion. People who saw the crowd must have thought that some celebrity was about to arrive. And indeed, she was. To us who were gathered, it was the most important meeting in months, with special meaning. It was like the prodigal son coming home, or an athlete who has won a medal. Even more than that, it was another step in watching a miracle unfold in God's mighty plan.

The Fast Forward group from the church, of which Roxanne had been a part, had attempted to make her feel welcome when she came home. What greeted her was a long "Welcome Home" sign made of newsprint about fifteen meters in length. Her friends were there to hold it up. But they were also there to see her. That is what mattered to her.

In our telephone conversations, Nettie and I had often talked about the side effects of the drugs that Roxanne was on. Now in the tense moments of waiting, I was uncertain of my reaction. Would it be noticeable? Of all the people in attendance, I had seen her last. She had still looked like herself when I last saw her. I refused to believe that the effects would be that obvious.

Finally, the moment arrived. I could see them both, but Roxanne was so different. She had lost a lot of weight. Her hair was thin. She now had heavy, chubby cheeks and dark eyebrows. Prednisone, in particular, left its mark on the patient. She had beautiful long eyelashes. She became the envy of many, who wished they had longer ones. This change had happened since I left London just over two months ago.

I struggled within myself not to show disappointment. For the moment it was important that our family was complete, that health had been restored, to some degree and at some cost. Feelings and emotions could mend over time.

There were few dry eyes as sixty people waited their turn for a hug. It was more than a reunion; it was a quiet thanksgiving service. I'm certain that many prayers of thanks were offered in those few moments, as people reflected on the previous months' experiences. There before them stood a teenager who, six months earlier, had been healthy; in the meantime, she had been at death's door. Their prayers had helped nurse her back to health.

For Nettie, it was the culmination of months of strain and stress, in which she had been responsible for the on-the-spot decisions. Finally, she was in a position to share that responsibility, or even to hand it over to me. Her relief was so apparent amid the tears of joy. The strain of tension had been so strong for so long that it was obvious that she would simply *crash* from exhaustion. But at least she could do this in the comfort of her own home.

For the moment, our family was complete and together. We celebrated as Shelly served us supper that evening. What a treat!

Serious illness in the hospital is manageable because the medical staff is always there when needed. Such sickness in the home, with one's doctor thousands of kilometers away, does have quite a different effect. For the first while, we sat on pins and needles: How do you feel? Is there a fever? Do you have pain? Are you sure you can do it? How did you sleep last night?

Do the questions sound as if we were nervous? There was no doubt about it. We were!

Trips to the hospital came frequently, first to introduce this new human specimen to the Calgary staff, and also for frequent tests. The staff was cautious, not willing to take any risks in allowing the possibility of rejection. After all, the staff at London had performed a medical miracle that was not possible in Calgary. Now that patient had been given back to them to continue treatment and monitor convalescence.

Before long, our fears became realities as she began to spike a fever and show symptoms of nausea. Both were signs of rejection, and they concerned us. But fever was controlled with Tylenol, and most of these bouts were brief. We dismissed the signs as part of the process of recovery. But the medical staff was more concerned. Their approach was that "if there is a fever, there must be a cause." They proceeded to seek that cause.

With the approach of the long weekend in May, we decided that it would be a good time to spend at the cottage at Parkland Beach. Roxanne was willing to go and looked forward to it, particularly since she had such a keen interest in the little things in life. Everything around her had taken on a new beauty, and she enjoyed this radiance as she enjoyed life itself.

A dream of mine developed as we struggled through the hardships of transplant life. Would it be possible for Roxanne to enjoy the beautiful surroundings of cottage and beach again? Perhaps at one point there had been some doubt. Now it was reality. She suggested the walk to the beach, and for me it was another time of thanksgiving. God had proven to me again that his healing power goes beyond my imagination.

While we were at the cottage, Roxanne became ill again, with numerous symptoms that we feared. It was time for further medical investigation to be done. Test after test was carried out that week, in hope of finding the root of the problems. Something was wrong.

According to Dr. Klassen, who had become one of Roxanne's doctors because of his involvement in kidney transplants, there was a dark spot in the area of the liver. His diagnosis: an abscess. In consultation with other specialists at Foothills Hospital as well as telephone contact with Dr. Wall in London, they soon established the plan for her to return to London.

A return to the transplant hospital is a psychological letdown for any recipient patient and family. It was a setback, and not good news. For us at home it was depressing. They left on our wedding anniversary. We had no time to celebrate this event. It was the day before Roxanne's graduation from grade 12. And they would probably not be back before Lyndon left for Germany on his summer missions assignment.

Roxanne had come home feeling reasonably well. She was leaving in a wheelchair. It is difficult to keep the spirits up under those circumstances.

Modern technology was good to us. Before she left, Roxanne was fortified with antibiotics. With all the arrangements made, she left the bed in Foothills Hospital and was readmitted to her bed in University Hospital in just eight hours. Flight attendants and travel personnel were understanding as well. Credit cards were a help, and so was the confidence that the government would come through with reimbursements.

Just being in London did not improve the situation, and her condition gradually deteriorated. Even that staff's expert knowledge was limited. Roxanne suffered constant nausea, fever, pain; these are not pleasant conditions for anyone. On top of such symptoms, constant tests had to be performed to get to the root of the matter. Emotionally, the separation from home, the return to London (where they had bade farewell), and the uncertainty of what was wrong and what might happen, drained any enthusiasm and strength that both of them had.

I sensed this heaviness, and decided it was a good time for me to pay them a visit, regardless of the fact that they had just left home a week ago. It was crucial to me that I be there for moral support. I made flight and family care arrangements. John and Tina once again stepped in to fill the need. What a blessing they were—doing this for us!

One of the tests done for Roxanne was to attempt to drain off the infection by inserting a long needle directly into the liver, in order to drain the bile that seemed to be infected. The liver was functioning; that was not the problem. I was amazed by the amount of fluid that was being drawn off. It was bile, so the liver must be producing. What then could be wrong? Some comments left questions in our mind. "No," they said, "it isn't rejection; it's an infection. There is debris floating around in the fluid." What might that mean?

Day after day the routine seemed unchanged—fever, nausea, pain, frustration, and seeming lack of progress. Then the cycle would repeat itself. "We're waiting for the infection to subside so we can see the biliary tree better. Then we can clear the blockage and she will be on her way to recovery." But there was no such turn of events, and there came a time when the doctors, too, shook their head as to the next move.

What was that next move? Surgery. They needed to get to the heart of the matter, in this case, the liver of the matter, to see what the real problem was. They had to "bring it out into the sunshine," as the saying goes. Although rejection had been ruled out, there was something amiss in the liver, and exploratory surgery would produce an explanation.

Roxanne had come to realize that this might be the only way out of a long tunnel which she had dreaded for so long. She actually began to look forward to it, not as a joyful occasion, but rather as a relief to her suffering over so many months.

Surgery was set for Saturday, June 20, but as is often the case, some emergencies take precedence over others. Saturday came and went with no surgery. Nettie and Roxanne took solace in the fact that someone else in desperate need was being helped. But the pressure of the situation weighed heavily on them. Tears often became an outlet for their frustration.

God reveals himself intimately at times such as this, and in various ways. Songs are a common vehicle of this revelation. In those hours before surgery, while they idly flicked through the TV channels, words sung by the Hymn Sing choir ministered to them in a soothing way. First the words of one song found its way into their room and into their hearts: "Blessed assurance, Jesus is mine! O what a foretaste of glory divine!" They could identify with such assurance.

A second song was sung: "We shall behold him." At this point our faith was sagging. Would she perhaps see the God she believed in sooner than we expected, or was this a message to tell us that we would, in fact, behold the beauty of God in a real and practical way in healing?

We heard another song: "His eye is on the sparrow, and I know he watches me." The words of the song were taken from Matthew 6:26-31 and 10:29-31. What a blessed consolation! If God took care of the sparrow, which seemed so worthless, would he not much more look after our personal needs, even if they seemed so insurmountable to us at the moment?

The call came: "Bring Roxanne down to the OR." She was ready to go. This would be the first step to recovery, despite its painfulness. Nettie followed her through the hallways to the operating room, where she saw her being placed onto a stretcher and wheeled away by trusted nurses, doctors, and anesthetists.

For the moment we were at peace. The problem would be analyzed, the infection flushed out, and recovery would be the next step. In a week or so, we would have our bouncing gal back again.

11

The time passed slowly. I waited at home for word from Nettie assuring me of the success of the operation. After all, Dr. Wall had said that although this was a serious operation, there was no need to be afraid or to call Dad to the bedside. However, sometimes one's mind plays tricks. When I expected the call by 9:00 p.m. and had not heard by 11:00 p.m., I begin to imagine the worst. This was equivalent to 1:00 a.m. in London. But our faith assured us that everything would be alright.

Dr. Wall came out of the operating room and summoned Nettie into the quiet room alone. This was not a good sign. Friends had rallied around her all day, and some stayed into the wee hours of the morning. That's what friendships are made of.

Nettie heard the dreaded words: "The operation was unsuccessful. There is no biliary tree; it has totally disintegrated and therefore cannot function." That was why they couldn't find it on the X-ray.

"Maybe it is a form of local rejection. We can't be

certain yet. There was nothing there to repair. We need a new liver—fast! The transplant coordinator has been notified and is already working on locating a new organ. Ask your husband to be on the next plane to London."

That's how good doctors perform. They do their best medically, then they stand by the family and give the straight facts, without pulling punches or making impossible promises. Their direction was set, and they knew where they were going.

When they broke the news, Nettie had to face the facts alone, without family. Months of pent-up emotion and frustration—which were supposed to culminate in a success story—began to break at the words of a man we had learned to trust so deeply. So did her composure.

Kathy and Jean must have known that they were needed there that night. Their friendship had gone beyond their responsibility. They were staff members, but both had taken a personal interest in Roxanne and her family, and they stood by at the moment when they were needed. Nothing could stem the tide of emotion. It was necessary, and had to be released. The tears we had seen, the sobs we had heard coming from the quiet room, the embraces, the attempts to comfort, now were ours. We had seen the reactions of others who had lost loved ones. Would ours be any different?

Six months after Roxanne had become ill, she was back at square one; she needed a liver immediately, or it would be too late. In our minds it was an unthinkable dilemma, far too insurmountable for us to fathom. It weighed so heavily on us. Yet it was possible in God's eyes.

It was 11:30 p.m. in Calgary when Nettie called. She was calm and spoke with composure. The initial flood of grief had subsided with that outburst, and a bold new look at the situation had helped her settle down. But the fact remained. I was to be on a plane as soon as possible.

Life at home was put on hold once again. School wasn't over, but colleagues could step in for me as they had done before. Others had substituted for me so many times before, and I had to realize that my jobs could be done by others again. Life could go on without me. I worked until 4:00 a.m. updating files and writing instructions so that my tasks could be passed on to others. And they would do admirable work.

With preparations out of the way, and with a ticket graciously provided by a business friend, I was on my way to London a third time. But I was apprehensive. Was God going to answer our prayer and heal her, or was I going to say good-bye to my daughter? That answer for the moment was based on faith in a God who could heal.

My faith was definitely being stretched. Had I not taken God at his promise when he said "Ask and you will receive"? We certainly were not receiving; instead, we were set back six months in fulfillment of our prayer requests. What did God have in mind? Was my faith not strong enough? Was this to be another way of giving it substance?

An area I felt needed to be addressed with Roxanne was the fact that the medical staff, too, might be running out of options. The body is strong, but when it is racked with fever and pain and illness over such a long period of time, its resistance is low. Each succeeding operation, let alone each succeeding transplant, becomes more difficult. How much can the body take?

Yet, was it my responsibility as a father to suggest that hope for survival was fading when in fact she was still full of fight and unwilling to give up? When I stood at her bedside, I realized that through her tears, she still had the hope necessary to hang in there one more time, endure what had to be endured, and pray for healing.

What we really needed this time was a compatible organ so that the body could function more to recover and to heal than to ward off rejection. Her faith and spunk were an inspiration to us.

Roxanne was instantly put on a code 0, which indicated urgency. The transplant team did its job well, and we were awakened the next morning by a call to let us know that the retrieval team was on its way to pick up a new organ in Harrisburg, Pennsylvania. This one, we were told, was a perfect match, in size and blood type. Our spirits soared, as did our prayers of thanksgiving. Yes, God was hearing and he was answering, but in his time.

There was hope. A new liver was coming on wings of hope. In the meantime, more pain and waiting. But such pain seemed more bearable today because there was a new ray of hope. We rushed to the hospital to spend a little more time with her. Surgery was scheduled for 12:00 noon. Our visits would have to be earlier. It was important to be there. As they wheeled her by, we whispered our support to her, and in her face we saw that ray of hope.

Transplant surgery is long and taxing. It was more than twelve hours from the time we saw her being wheeled into the operating room until we saw her in intensive care after surgery. Overcome with fatigue we graciously accepted the hospitality suite as our personal waiting room again and promptly fell asleep.

At 4:00 p.m. we were awakened by sirens outside. It was a police cruiser. We later learned that at that very moment the precious liver was being carried through the rush-hour traffic from the airport to the hospital by police escort. This was another reason to be thankful.

Restlessness can be a problem at the best of times. Under such circumstances it is worse. We paced the floor, drank coffee, looked at the clock, tried to read, listened for footsteps in the hallway—first in one sequence, then in reverse order, as we had done during the first transplant, five months earlier.

With the passing of time our imagination was hyperactive: Why was it taking so long? Could there be complications? Was there too much infection? Could they flush out the infection to avoid any further complications? An organ transplant may take seven, eight, or nine hours, but we were approaching the twelve-hour mark. Was everything alright?

Those trusty footsteps in the hall, the firm hand on the door, came at last. The familiar frame of Dr.

Wall appeared with encouraging words. The operation was successful. The organ was a perfect match in size and blood type. The infection had been localized in the area of the old liver and as a result they were confident that any bugs that existed had been flushed out. Praise God for medical confidence!

We were allowed to see her at about 2:00 a.m. The nurses were constantly monitoring her vitals. Blood pressure, breathing, pulse, and comfort are all so important at this stage. A person on life-support systems is not a pretty sight, but for us, beauty at this point was secondary. There was life, and there was hope. What more could we expect?

At first Roxanne's recovery was slow. Normally a postoperative wake-up period is only several hours. At noon the next day, some twelve hours later, there was still no response, and the medical staff was noticeably concerned. There was no twitch, no involuntary movement of any sort.

Back they went to the books and the records, to peruse the possible causes. Meanwhile, we parents stood by, held her hand, stroked her face, and talked to her, trying to help her understand that we were there. Nurses continued to want us in the room. Perhaps Roxanne was aware of our presence, but could not respond to it.

Late that afternoon a nurse thought she determined a change in blood pressure rate when we walked in after a break. Excitement mounted as we waited. Then Nettie thought she felt her hand squeezed ever so slightly when she asked Roxanne to do so. It was true; Roxanne was responding—only a little, but nonetheless it was awareness. With repeated encouragement, we were able to get considerable reaction by the time we left for the night.

What was the reason for her delay? Likely it was the combination of drugs, the heavy dose of anesthetics from two surgeries only a few days apart, and her intake of cyclosporine. Such a simple explanation, but such a concern in the crisis!

Roxanne's determination seemed obvious. She was resolved to waste little time in getting better. Within two days she was off the respirator. In three days she was out of ICU. Both came as a surprise to us. There seemed to be no holding back.

Pain seemed to be the only thing with which she constantly needed to contend. The doctors responded by giving her a demand pump for morphine. They hoped that by self-administering morphine Roxanne would have less pain, allowing for more rest and quicker recovery.

There were setbacks, tears, pain, and heartbreak, but Roxanne was healing and on the road of progress. The future began to look brighter, and the picture of recuperation seemed to have numerous rays of sunshine etched in and mingled with the shadows.

For Roxanne it continued to be a round of pain, nausea, and frustration. For us as parents, it was encouragement and positive reinforcement. Bible reading and prayer with Roxanne was still a highlight every day as we shared ideas about God's love and answered prayer.

Gwen and Corinne, who by this time were beginning to wonder what Mom looked like, made another trip to London, again courtesy of business friends. Plans were for them to stay two weeks, after which I too would come home and get them ready for Camp Evergreen before I went to Edmonton to bury myself in marking grade 9 social studies papers.

But what about housing while we were there? We were staying at the Hunnifords' at no cost to us. Could we be so brazen as to bring a whole family into their home? An answer came sooner than we expected. Frank and Jean asked us to house-sit for them while they went to the east coast for a holiday. What a godsend! We moved into their house for a two-week period and lived like royalty.

Holiday time cannot be denied. Hospital surroundings do not make for a good camping or sightseeing environment for adults, let alone teenagers. How long can one count staples on an incision, or find new ways to read a monitor, or go for meaningful walks down corridors, or find imaginative ways to enjoy the food in the cafeteria? It wasn't long before we explored Storybook Gardens in London and Canada's Wonderland in Toronto. Both days were spent in relaxation and enjoyment, as well as in relief away from the hospital setting. The only thing which made the hospital more attractive was its airconditioning during the heat wave, which topped thirty-six degrees Celsius.

Roommates are an important part of a patient's life. They can make life bearable and perhaps even borderline enjoyable at times. Roxanne had her share of roommates during her eight months in hospital. Some she learned to appreciate with deep sincerity.

Lynne was such a person. She had her liver transplant in June 1986 and was back for a checkup and further diagnosis. Both girls were young and had so much in common that it wasn't hard to develop a close bond. Deep and lasting friendships are formed under such difficult circumstances.

My first encounter with Lynne was one evening during our devotional time with Roxanne. We had read from the Bible together with Terry, her roommate. When we were ready to pray, Roxanne invited Lynne to join us as we prayed. She had just dropped in for a prebedtime visit and was sitting nearby.

All five of us held hands as we committed each of the girls to the Lord for healing, recovery, and inner strength. Later the two girls became roommates, and their prayer for each other continued. Another friendship had developed that would last for a lifetime. Lynne and her family were added to our prayer list.

Progress continued to be rapid. Before the girls and I left for home, Roxanne had been given several day passes for supper engagements, not without frustration and concern, but nonetheless a measure of freedom. Before long we would need an expanded repertoire of eateries to keep up our interest. Such visits were also cumbersome. We needed to go at Roxanne's speed and allow her time to go through the painstaking procedure of taking a half-dozen different medications right after supper. I'm sure that several waitresses must have suspected drug addiction.

We left her in fairly good condition, as the three

of us departed for Calgary, but nausea, pain, and diarrhea began to take its toll. Recuperation was delayed. Test after test was done to attempt to determine the cause. Scan tests, culture tests, blood tests, X-rays, marrow tests, and fluid tests all led to the same conclusion: There was no major problem. She must have a virus, that catchall word which seemed to us to cover everything that could not be otherwise diagnosed.

Whatever it was, she continued to lose weight till she was a mere eighty-four pounds. When I returned to London, I could almost reach my thumb and middle finger around the calf of her leg. I playfully called her "my little Biafran." If there was a desire for food, it would not stay down. If she did eat, it was only a few mouthfuls. Finally it came to what the doctors had threatened to do for so long: put a feeding tube down her nose.

A feeding tube down the nose, when oral food won't stay down? I was skeptical. Before long I was convinced. It was a way to get the stomach to settle down and begin to handle larger amounts of food. Larger amounts, indeed! Before long she was getting fifty, then seventy-five cubic centimeters of food formula per hour. For a body that is not used to digesting large amounts of food, that was a lot. Now she really took on the physique of a starving person—a body of skin and bones and a distended stomach. But it did the trick. It gave her the necessary food, while it prepared her stomach to take regular food.

I was in London for the fourth time. Being on

125

summer holidays, I was more available to travel now than when school resumed. I arrived to see her sick and nauseous. Before I left, however, the feeding tube was working. She was given a day pass again, they pulled the tube, and off we went, a wheelchair in the back seat, scouting out southern Ontario.

Something had happened in Roxanne's life. As we wheeled her into a rose garden in suburban London, she leaned forward and smelled each blossom she could reach. Then she asked me to wheel her closer to the next patch of flowers. We watched the squirrels scamper from tree to tree, and we enjoyed the newfound freedom of the outdoors, which had suddenly also taken on an aura of deep beauty.

We traveled down a country road in rural Ontario, between fields of corn. She was overcome by a lovely cornfield, the lively farm animals grazing, and even the accompanying smell of the farmyards. This was life in its radiance and fullness. And she was alive and well and enjoying every minute as she savored it with a new set of senses.

Then she became aware of another sensation—hunger. The tube was gone. A crutch for so many days, it was no longer there. Now *real food* must replace it. A trip to McDonalds was the first stop in proving this new step. A Big Mac and Coke quickly replaced the contents of the feeding tube and with no ill effects. The next day it was to Hunnifords' for supper, where two pork chops and trimmings were hardly sufficient to satisfy the hunger pangs. If people on cyclosporine had large appetites, this was indeed the first sign.

When I left London to go back to Calgary and work, there was a confidence that perhaps, finally, most hurdles had been overcome. A few more days in the hospital, a few more day passes, then a discharge with only visits for blood tests and physiotherapy.

It was a time to savor reclaimed experience of the senses. First it was a ride down the Thames River on the *Tinkerbell*, then off to Stratford to see *Romeo and Juliet*, then to Grand Bend to see *Brigadoon*, then to Kitchener to drive through the African Safari. She was not to be denied the freedom and expression of herself which she had missed for so long. Although she was not strong, with her determination, the wheelchair, and Nettie keeping her in tow, they blazed new trails together. Niagara Falls was also on the list, but time ran out.

The welcome words from the doctor finally came: "You can plan to go home on Friday." As gratifying as the words were, they also carried with them uneasiness in cutting ties with what had been home for almost eight months. It meant that Calgary doctors would have to become involved. Cherished ties and friendships made in London under trying circumstances would now have to be left behind. Those friendships were deeply valued because of the way people gave of themselves.

The day for which we had waited so long finally came. The aircraft was winging its way home, bearing precious cargo: a young body with a new life, Roxanne, and her mother, Nettie.

No, the concerns were not over, but life would begin to settle down to a normal pace. Savoring the bittersweet would be worth it; the horizon was beautifully tinted with promise. Hope had become a reality. Prayer had been answered.

12

Our ordeal stimulated us to reflect on our faith. Did God answer prayer for us, or was it simply a matter of routine circumstances? If the Lord did answer prayer, why was it in such a roundabout way, and why did Roxanne have to suffer so? We had always been taught that God answers prayer; now where was the proof? Why would *our* chosen path be so much shorter and easier than his?

These questions plied our minds in the months that followed the reuniting of our family in Calgary. We searched for answers in Scripture and in our experiences.

As one trusting in the divine hand of God leading in the daily life of the Christian, I believed that everything which passed our way in life was either directed by God, allowed by him, or perhaps even sent by him. God is a part of everyday life and can be experienced in intimate ways. In attempting to organize my thoughts for myself, I divided them into several categories.

First, there is *God's directive will,* or his creative will—his desire to create things good and beautiful. At the end of each day of creation, the Bible in Genesis 1 says, "God saw that it was good"!

From a scientific, medical, or technological point of view this is intriguing. After all the research which has been done, mankind is still at a loss to explain the functioning of some parts of the universe, or the body, or the laws of nature. From a believer's point of view, it may be breathtaking, but it isn't hard to accept. There is a Creator who can do amazing things.

In all his power, God simply made everything and was able to say of that creation, "It is good!" Take the intricacy of the universe, the beauty and majesty of a mountain scene (Psalm 19), or the medical wonder of the body (Psalm 139:13-16). One can see that a powerful Creator has been at work. In other words, it was God's will that the world should rotate, and that the body should function in harmony with all its intricate systems.

Then something went wrong. Man and woman were placed on the earth to care for it and enjoy it. Through these human beings, sin entered the world and things began to deteriorate when they fell into sin by choice (Genesis 2–3). Hard work and perspiration became the order of the age. Pain, sorrow, disappointment, and distortion of relationships were introduced. Deterioration and death became a conscious part of life.

Humankind had made a choice, and God, in his wisdom, had accepted their decision to go their own way. They broke fellowship with their Maker and caused him pain and suffering. This is where *God's permissive will* came in. He refused to force them to live against their own decision. And if some of the consequences were painful, God allowed these to happen as well.

Now a distorted cycle had been introduced. When a person was born, his life of joy was punctuated with pain and hardship. Death loomed on the horizon, inevitable. For some, the dying came at the end of a full life; for others, life was ever so short. The process of dying included some ugly and painful experiences, made more bleak by sinful separation from the Lord. God had spoken. Creation now had a measure of deterioration and distortion. The good news is that God through Christ is bringing redemption to all of creation (Romans 8:18-25).

There is, however, an area of God's will which he claims as King of the universe. It might be called *God's absolute will.* If we could effectively challenge God on his actions, he would not be sovereign, and God.

Several passages back this biblical principle. The Lord in Exodus 33:19 says, "I will make all my goodness pass before you, and will proclaim before you my name 'The Lord'; and I will be gracious to whom I will be gracious, and will show mercy on whom I will show mercy."

As a start toward his purpose to bless all nations (Genesis 12:3), God had a chosen people, Israel, whom he called his own. No one dared ask him regarding the validity of that choice; it was simply

his right as sovereign God. It was based on a covenant set with Abraham and renewed in succeeding
generations.

In the path of that choice were some casualties:
Some were due to human decisions, as when Pharaoh hardened his heart (Exodus 9:34) or some Israelites murmured against God and had to take the
consequences (Numbers 11:1). Some were due to
God's planning and action, as when God hardened
Pharaoh's heart (Exodus 10:1) or overcame the Egyp-
tian army (Exodus 14:19-25). Time after time the
mercy and grace of God was shown, in his goodness
to his people. If you were God, how long could *you*
keep patience with a nation that constantly broke its
part of the covenant?

God's mercy extends to all people. But some persons open to receiving his mercy seem more than
others to be on the receiving end of hurt, pain, suffering, financial loss, or even death. God does not
owe anyone his goodness or an explanation for his
actions. The sun shines and the rain falls on both the
just and the unjust (Matthew 5:45).

Another area in which human beings cannot
second-guess God is in the decisions God makes to
stop some people in their tracks, or to "blot them
out." In other words, his mercy comes to an end at
one point and people must face the music. In
Genesis 6:7, the Lord says, "I will blot out man
whom I have created from the face of the ground,
man and beast and creeping things and birds of the
air, for I am sorry that I have made them."

God sticks to his Word. The story continues: Noah

and his family were saved from the disastrous flood, but the rest of humankind was not. Why was Noah chosen? He "found favor in the eyes of the Lord" (Genesis 6:8).

What about the others? Did they not find that favor with God? They experienced the consequences of their evil actions. "And the Lord was sorry that he had made man on the earth, and it grieved him to his heart" (Genesis 6:6). God's grace had simply run out. He saw the wickedness, and determined that it had run its course. It was time for a day of reckoning. No one could dissuade him from his purpose in the impending doom.

True, there was still opportunity for repentance while the ark was in construction. During that time Noah was busy preaching (2 Peter 2:5) with his carpentry as well as his lifestyle and words. Not many people have a boat that size in their backyard. It was bound to be a conversation piece. There was time to repent. But that time of grace ran out when the door of the ark closed and the rain began to fall.

That same approach is also true in the New Testament, where the message is clear. God is merciful (2 Peter 3:9), but there will come a day and a time when the grace of God will be over, and his judgment will begin. At such a time, no excuse will be sufficient to dissuade him from the possible results. God is indeed "slow to anger and abounding in steadfast love" (Psalm 103:8). Can God be faulted and accused of being unkind and unloving?

However, there is no excuse for one being unrecognizable because of not doing the Father's will

(Matthew 7:21), unprepared (Matthew 25:11-12), unproductive (Matthew 25:24-30), or not caring for the needy (Matthew 25:41-46). No alibi will stand before God on that day when the account is given. There are consequences for one's actions. God's decision is not open to question. Pleading after the fact will not change that decision.

One may try to argue with God to obtain an extension of life (Genesis 18; Deuteronomy 9; 2 Kings 20), but even if granted it is only a postponement of death. Everyone must face death, unless forestalled by the last trumpet (1 Corinthians 15). Some, unfortunately, are confronted by death while young. Others face it in midlife, or after a long and fruitful span of years. Why the difference?

Shall ailing persons argue for an extension? They may request it, but to demand it is out of order. Is God more angry with them than he is with me, in allowing me more time? No! God is sovereign, and his actions stand. God gives life, but he is able to forward his purpose even through an illness or death (Romans 8:28-39). When God calls in death, each of us must answer, and Jesus shows the way by commiting his spirit to the Father (Luke 23:46).

Let us reflect further on *God's permissive will.* As some things come our way, God allows us to experience them as a part of a much larger plan. When disasters occur, families and communities are involved in the attending hurt. Disasters happen constantly. Do they happen in Colombia or Mexico because those people deserve to suffer more than others do? I think not (Luke 13:1-5). Our family did not deserve to suffer more than others in our group of acquaintances. Nor were we more prepared to take it on the chin than others. There was a deeper purpose.

If God, as Creator and Sustainer of the universe, allows disasters to happen (such as earthquakes, hurricanes, floods, and tornadoes), or even sends them, then people will also get hurt in the process. He does not necessarily choose locations with no population to pinpoint an earthquake. Can you imagine a hurricane cutting a path through America, but dodging population centers as it goes? He is the Creator.

God has set forces and patterns in motion by which the earth operates. He is responsible for heat and cold, high-pressure areas and low ones, as well as the resulting winds. But God does not apologize for the death and destruction that comes in their wake. The dynamic patterns of creation which God put into motion are running their course under his unsleeping supervision. And God has given us intelligence to plan to minimize the ill effects of natural forces.

God even allows manmade or man-related disasters to happen. Wars, crimes, murder, terrorism, as well as alcohol-related accidents, happen with amazing frequency. Can God stop them? Yes, he can, but he doesn't. They are the results of choices which human beings have made and which bear consequences. God has allowed violence to happen because some persons chose that. In the process, innocent people get hurt.

Thus arises the criticism by many that a God of

love would not do such things. But people don't always respond to love, and sometimes God must resort to seemingly unloving things to get the message of his love through to them.

Why does God not stop such cruel activity? Why did he not stop Herod from beheading John the Baptist? Herod had made a decision, and the consequences were not pretty (Mark 6:14-29). Why did God allow Christians in the early church to be martyred so brutally? Sometimes he uses that type of a prod to get Christians on with their tasks. Persecution uprooted believers so that the gospel would be preached wherever they were scattered (Acts 7:54-8:4). Out of death and sorrow can come something good. An experience is deepened or a lesson is learned, albeit at great expense.

Some might argue that Satan is sometimes involved. He would love to play havoc in a person's life. This certainly was the case in Job's situation (Job 1:6-12; 2:1-7). But Satan was forced to stay within limits. In the first chapter, he was not allowed to touch Job's health. In the second, he was not allowed to touch his life.

Job was used as an object lesson, to show that Satan's power is limited, as well as to show Job's friends how they needed to bring their lives into line. The interesting finale to the story is that Job came through the experience an older, wiser, and more godly person because of his experiences. He said, "I know that my Redeemer lives" (Job 19:25). The object lesson could be seen by Job, his friends, and millions of readers since.

As already mentioned, a natural disaster or a hurt such as we experienced does not necessarily happen to a given individual or family because they deserve it. Illness is not always the result of sin. True, sin brings its consequences and leaves its scars. For examples: drinking and driving can lead to death, smoking can lead to lung cancer, crime can lead to a jail term. . . . A child cannot play on the highway repeatedly and not get hurt.

But when the blind man was brought to Jesus, his disciples asked him this very question: "Who sinned, this man or his parents?" His response: "It was not that this man sinned, or his parents, but that the works of God might be made manifest in him" (John 9:1-3).

There was a deeper result. It was allowed so that God's glory should be seen in the circumstances. Can it be seen in blindness? Yes indeed! A blind person in accepting the handicap can praise God. Many bedridden invalids smiling through their pain have brought glory to God. Sharing in that situation can be uplifting for others.

Yet in John 9 it is not in the blindness, but in the healing, that God looks for his glory; the man became a follower of Jesus after he was healed. Perhaps the miraculous sign of a cure through Jesus would lead others to become followers as well.

On the other hand, God may simply bring experiences our way. When Jesus had his disciples go across the lake (Mark 6:45-52), he knew there would be contrary winds; yet he sent them. He saw their distress, but the storm was not stilled immediately.

He sent them into the storm, saw them struggling, and came to them, helping them deal with the situation. Jesus used the experience to mold them and cultivate their faith. He does similar things for us.

Sometimes God also sees fit to discipline us in order to shape us into something more useful. A little pruning can lead to more fruitfulness. Correction on the path can lead to a more exact course. Some fire can burn out the impurities of the raw ore. A little chipping can take away our rough edges. Molding can make us into a better and more usable vessel. A little discipline can lead to more respect for the Father, and a more mature outlook on life.

When hardship comes, it is good to know that there are limits. Daniel experienced these in the den of lions (Daniel 6:22). The lions had a case of lockjaw, and Daniel was spared. Similarly, you will not receive more than you are able to handle. If hardship does come in spurts, God's sustaining grace comes in bigger spurts. Had Roxanne's illness been fatal, I'm convinced that there would have been enough grace to face that situation as well. Thank God we didn't have to face that hardship.

The New Testament gives a promise of God setting limits: "No temptation has overtaken you that is not common to man. God is faithful, and he will not let you be tempted beyond your strength, but with the temptation will also provide the way of escape, that you may be able to endure it" (1 Corinthians 10:13).

We certainly found this to be true. When the hardship reached its breaking point, there was new strength, enough for the moment. Time after time, we found the grace necessary to sustain us.

So why is this not always the case? Why did God not put a stop to the beheading of John the Baptist? Why do so many people have to die, when there is a promise of limits to suffering? It is a part of God's larger plan, a plan that we don't always understand (Isaiah 55:8-9). Sometimes we simply don't follow God's thought process. We see only the tangled patchwork on the underside of the quilt, rather than the beauty from above.

Christianity spread due to persecution. Christians were pried loose from their security and scattered abroad, sharing their faith as they went. New believers would not have embraced Christianity so readily if they had not seen the devotion and fervency that went with the suffering and martyrdom. People turn to God in crisis situations, and he responds marvelously. Many feel they don't need God when there is no crisis. Yet God is always there, not only in times of need, but likewise in the quietness of reverence and worship.

Bearing hardship is also a way of showing God's strength through us. If we thought a cure came only through our ability, expertise, or medical technology, God would not get the credit. Yet what have we, skills or otherwise, which we did not receive from the Creator? (1 Corinthians 4:7.) God blesses the healing efforts; when our ability is thwarted, he fills the gap and receives glory.

Credit is certainly due the medical staff at University Hospital, but God worked through them and was able to outheal them. Our choice was not to experience the ordeal of eight months. We would have opted for a quick diagnosis and only a brief illness, or better still, no illness at all. But God had other plans.

Full health was not restored to Roxanne quickly, or without long-lasting effects, as in the case of the apostle Paul: "A thorn was given me in the flesh, a messenger of Satan. . . . Three times I besought the Lord about this, that it should leave me; but he said to me, 'My grace is sufficient for you, for my power is made perfect in weakness' " (2 Corinthians 12:7-10).

What if . . . ? What if the liver had deteriorated too fast, and the result would have been death? What if time would have run out before the team found a suitable liver? We know of several families that stood at a graveside of their loved one who had received a transplant. What if God would have refused to remove the thorn that was there? Would we have been able to accept such an answer?

Mine is a speculative reply: in spite of the difficulty, I am confident that the grace would have been there. With God's help, some of it through our network of supporting Christian friends, we would have been able to endure it without losing our faith or our mind—and even to learn from it. He sustained us previously when we buried loved ones. He would do it again.

If our response is to hope in God, experiences such as ours can bring people closer to God.

As with a deadly wound in my body. . . .

Hope in God; for I shall again praise him,
my help and my God. (Psalm 42:10-11)

If we do not become bitter, we are open to receive God's comfort. We have nowhere else to turn. We cling to hope that we will be able to praise God "in the midst of the congregation" (Psalm 22:22).

Disappointment and despair have a way of helping us focus on the things in life that really count, things that have eternal value. Rather than spending time on trivial matters, our thoughts are turned heavenward and toward more life-affirming human relationships. Our actions take on a more serious approach.

As a result, the Lord is able to work in our lives in greater detail, dredging out those areas which are unsuitable, and nurturing dormant dimensions which need stimulus for growth. Deeper sorrow allows for more depth of maturity to occur.

Saints of the ages have trod this way before us:

Even though I walk through the valley of the shadow
of death,
I fear no evil;
for thou art with me;
thy rod and thy staff,
they comfort me. (Psalm 23:4)

In this you rejoice, though now for a little while you
may have to suffer various trials, so that the genuineness of your faith, more precious than gold which
though perishable is tested by fire, may redound to
praise and glory and honor at the revelation of Jesus
Christ. (1 Peter 1:6-7)

Hardship also helps people to identify with the hurts of others. Having shed tears in the past period has given me a new awareness of the tears and hurts of others. Sharing with others why we appear to be so strong can only lead to giving God the glory. In our own strength such experiences would be impossible to endure. That brings us back to the concept of the object lesson. Our experience was there so that others may benefit from it. We have been sensitized and strengthened to be able to help carry the burdens of others going through a similar ordeal.

Paul says it so well:

> Blessed be . . . the Father of mercies and God of all comfort, who comforts us in all our affliction, so that we may be able to comfort those who are in any affliction, with the comfort with which we ourselves are comforted by God. (2 Corinthians 1:3-4)

For this reason we could empathize with the hurts of others and add them and their needs to our prayer list. We could embrace and shed tears with a person who had lost a loved one.

It led us to take time from visiting Roxanne to attend a funeral of Bob, who did not recover from transplant surgery. It gave us the courage to support Sheila through suspense as she waited through Ray's transplant without other family members present. It led us to pray with Lynne and Terry as we shared with them the reason why we had confidence in our God. Their hurts had become our hurts, and we trust that we may have helped to lighten the load ever so slightly.

During the illness, the time dragged on endlessly. It seemed like such a long eight months. But the harshness of the illness and the separation will fade over the years, and that period will shrink to what seems to be such a small interval. Time has a way of healing the hurts. The scraped knee which was painful for so long in your childhood, now is scarcely remembered.

An oyster has a unique way of reacting to irritation and pain. When a grain of sand gets into the shell and lodges in its body, it causes irritation. The oyster responds by secreting a liquid to protect itself from the intrusion. That secretion hardens around the foreign object and forms a beautiful pearl.

Out of the pain comes something priceless, beautiful, and enhancing. That is the way God meant it to be. The pain, hardship, and suffering which occurs can lead to something more beautiful for others to enjoy. That is the way we experienced it.

We were being *cultured through pain.* We were like a diamond in the rough. The value was there, but the beauty was not complete. Some chipping and polishing and shaping had to be done. Some of the excess dross had to be removed in order that more of the real value and beauty could be revealed. That process is still continuing.

How did we make it through the hardship? It was as if God were carrying us through the most difficult experiences. It was through the meaningfulness of songs, cards, phone calls, and actions of friends that we were uplifted. Such support is so necessary and so reassuring. Many such gestures brought tears of

143

joy and thanksgiving. We were able to learn a tenderness and sensitivity to others in similar need.

Songs help to fill many needs at such times. The words to one song that we often heard were: "I am the Lord that healeth thee." What a reassuring thought in the midst of our struggles. Words from another song expressed confidence as well: "I don't know what's around the corner, Lord, but I know that you'll be there." Each encouragement was readily accepted and applied as needed.

It was like the picture of the sands of time, in which two sets of footprints, God's and a pilgrim's, suddenly become one. In searching for an explanation, the pilgrim is told that the footprints did not merge because God left him alone. Instead, those were the times when the heavenly Father took the pilgrim on his own back and carried him through the hardship. Such was the sustaining help and love that we felt.

If Roxanne had not needed a transplant, our experience would not have been so rich. True, we would have enjoyed a life of ease and leisure, but we would not have been a part of the intimate lives of individuals as they experienced the pangs of illness and death. We would not have been in the ICU waiting room to participate in the joys and sorrows of others. We would not have been able to give those persons the reason why we had a measure of assurance in our lives that God was in charge.

Numerous people on flights to and from London would not have heard of our trust in God. Twenty transplant patients and their families would not have become a part of our lives. The Hunnifords would not have been introduced to us, let alone become so dear to us. Hundreds of people would not have been united as prayer partners in a common need.

Our lives have been changed by this experience. God had a purpose in mind. Not all of it is clear to me, but a few indicators are there. It is up to us to share with others of the comfort which we have experienced.

Did God answer prayer? Yes indeed he did! Not in our way, or in our time, or according to our understanding, but he answered prayer. Roxanne is vibrant evidence of this. Our lives have grown deeper as a result of this experience. Other lives have been touched. Today as we look back, we see not one, but many answers to prayer.

Praise the Lord!

Epilogue

At the time of writing, Roxanne is almost three years post transplant and is progressing well. She has completed her second year of training in physiotherapy at the University of Edmonton, with a difficult course load.

She has handled full-time employment along with an active social life. She lives away from home and must do her own laundry as well.

Those who question the quality of life provided by transplantation may be pleasantly surprised by the amount of energy Roxanne has. Other transplant recipients, similarly, have resumed their routine activities with little holding them back.

Although her immune system is suppressed, her rate of colds and illnesses has been minimal. She has ups and downs, as do we all, but in no way does she have only a subsistence quality of life. Her energy level is not thwarted, her courage is undaunted, and her love for beauty and appreciation has grown.

High on Roxanne's list of priorities is maintaining

contact with others who had liver transplants or who are experiencing apprehension as they wait for one. She loves to share her experiences for the sake of mutual encouragement.

It is important to Roxanne that others not see a transplant patient as one who has a lower quality of life. Hers is an active, full, and thankful life. She is a walking miracle.

In the back: Gwen, Nelson, Nettie, Henry
In the front: Shelly, Roxanne, Corinne, Lyndon

The Author

Henry Plett was born into a large family in the farming community of Gem, Alberta. He received his grade school and high school training in rural Alberta, after which he attended Alberta Mennonite Brethren (M.B.) Bible School in Coaldale for two years. Next he enrolled in the M.B. Bible College in Winnipeg, with remote thoughts of entering the ministry, stimulated by his father's repeated encouragement. During his senior year, he took the assignment of student pastor at Salem M.B. Church in Winnipeg. After graduation with a bachelor of theology degree, he enrolled in Sir Wilfrid Laurier University, Waterloo, Ontario, where he received his B.A. in history.

Plett then embarked on a teaching career, enrolling in the University of Calgary and receiving his bachelor of education degree. He began teaching for the Calgary Board of Education in 1969, where he is presently employed.

Plett has been active in his church throughout his adult life: teaching Sunday school, giving leadership to the Christian Service Brigade program, and working in the area of Christian education, lay involvement in the services, and on the board of elders and church executive. Presently he is a member of Dalhousie Community Church in Calgary.

Through this book Plett desires to let others share in the experiences he and his family went through. He wants others to sense God's message of love coming from this heart-wrenching ordeal.